"DuMort is an intriguing, attention-grabbing gaslamp horror fantasy. It evokes the dread and mystery of similar novels in the genre."

— JIM DORAN, AUTHOR OF FORLORN HARBOR

"DuMort is an intriguing, attention-grabbing gaslamp horror fantasy. It evokes the dread and mystery of similar novels in the genre."

— JIM DORAN, AUTHOR OF FORLORN HARBOR

DuMort

DuMort

MICHELLE TANG

GHOST ORCHID PRESS

DuMort

To Mom, Dad, Achi and Aimee

Chapter One

"In Mydalla, we do not speak of the dead."

SuChin left bruises around my neck, delicate blossoms budding purple beneath my skin which no amount of powder could hide. I hooked the stiff, high collar of my brocaded cloak closed and turned from my mirror. Hoped it would be too dark for mortal eyes to see the violence my sister's ghost had inflicted.

"I will be out for a few hours," I told Edgar, and waited for a sign that he cared. His eyes did not leave his book to glance at the gathering dusk; neither protest nor question passed his lips. And so, heavy-hearted, I passed through our front door.

The horses' shoes tapped a nervous rhythm, a secret code warning me to turn around. I rode through the streets, the carriage wheels bumping over wet cobblestone, lanterns that stained the evening fog a sickly yellow marking the distance. Rolling estates gave way to smaller, closer buildings, and soon a wall of narrow houses loomed over the road, their windows staring like unblinking eyes.

Beyond these structures, in the centre of Mydalla, the massive cathedral gazed upon the city like a benevolent god. The holy crematorium's four marble spires reached upwards to the skies, decanting precious souls into the heavens. Squatting alongside their brilliant glory like an ungainly sibling: the Bastille, constructed of black, rusting steel. It loomed like a threat.

Like a warning.

I turned my eyes from the ominous sight and steadied my breath.

When the carriage stopped, no one came from the private home to greet us. My driver clambered down to open my door himself. "Are you sure this is the right place, Mrs Braithwaite?" he asked as he helped me down, his tobacco-scented breath forming pale miasmas in the chill night air.

I nodded. Clenched my gloved hands around my skirts, but my disobedient fingers would not stop their trembling. My stomach churned, as if swirling to my fingers' rapid tempo. It was not fear that made my body shake, not really: it was hope.

But I had encountered hope before, followed closely by its child, despair.

"I was told he would be here." My voice was hoarse. "Stay here until I return, won't you?"

My cloak's gold threading caught the lantern light as I approached the house's entrance, the jewels scintillating like small stars. I would be overdressed, of course, but I had long learned it necessary. The house was a modest one, grey rough stone and black-lacquered door, the surname WILCOX carved into the lintel of the frame. The house was quiet, like the others I had passed, but dim illumination behind the windows revealed many silhouettes, and there was a sense of movement within.

I knocked with the blade of my fist. Miss Mina Kwan had never been meek, despite her humble beginnings, and Lady Mina Braithwaite was thrice as bold. A pause, evident even in the silence of the house, and then the faint vibration of footsteps neared the door. *Courage,* I girded myself, and fought the urge to neaten my hair or to smile.

A manservant greeted me, his gaze first falling on the midnight black of my hair, then lowering to my dark, slanted eyes and gentle nose; his own eyes widened as he scanned my rich clothing and fine jewels.

I lifted my chin; hoped my collar high enough to hide my throttled neck. "I understand the great occultist DuMort is a guest in this home this evening. It is imperative that I see him."

The servant shook his head politely. "Occultist? This is a law-abiding house, my lady. This is only a small gathering of the host's closest friends." There was a minuscule hesitation before he addressed me as lady, but I was well-used to hearing it.

I swallowed down my doubt and squared my shoulders beneath my cloak. "Then I am most grateful for the host's indulgence." I stepped forwards as if nothing would stop me, and the servant did not dare shut the door against my approach.

The night's cold air slipped past me to announce my arrival, and the people nearest the door turned towards me. There were no faces I recognised, no acquaintance to corroborate the rumours that would be birthed on this night, no friend to shame me back towards decency. I stalked from the foyer to what was a sitting room: a vase of flowers adorned a table between the guests seated on couch and twin armchairs, the flowers' colours muted into grey by the scant light. Shocked silence followed in my wake. My booted footsteps sounded unbearably loud against the wood floors. It was the only sound in the house, as if I were the ghost and the people around me were rendered mute by the horror of my intrusion. The rooms were dark, but a fire crackled in the hearth and candle flame flickered here and there, enough light to make the intricately carved baseboards and crown moulding visible. Framed paintings decorated the white walls, but I did not linger to admire them: there were too many bodies in the way.

I hesitated by the base of the curved stairway, unable to summon the courage to mount those steps to private bedrooms. Even I, in this most desperate of times, could not stoop to that level of impropriety.

DuMort had to be here. I had risked my husband's name with this action, faced certain humiliation, and it would all be for nought if I couldn't speak to the man.

A tall stranger approached me, surely the host himself. He spoke politely at first, but as I ignored his questions and stepped around him, he soon grew impatient and took hold of me.

He marched me back towards the door, past the unfamiliar faces which brightened with glee at my capture, and though my cheeks burned, my eyes did not stop their search.

There.

In the second room I'd rushed through, a sixth sense alerted me. I paused, halting the host mid-step lest he hurt me. My eyes were more accustomed to the dark by now, and the shape of a man coalesced behind the lone round table, behind the single candlestick.

It was DuMort.

I knew him at once, though the room was dim and he sat in the shadows. The poorly drawn posters that floated about town did not do him justice. In this room full of people, his very presence throbbed like a heart. A darkness emanated from him, a ravenous void that devoured everything, pulling gazes and people towards him. I could easily see him communing with the spirits: they, too, would be drawn by his magnetism.

I pulled away from the gentleman's firm grip on my shoulder and threw myself towards DuMort. He was the only one seated at the round table; his black garment merged with shadows that the candlelight could not chase away, until he seemed as vast as the room, ethereal as the night itself. The high collar of my cloak choked me as I lunged, until with a ripping of threads and gasps of disapproval, the fine garment fell away to hang, like a chastened child, from the host's hand.

"Please, sir," I said to the occultist, staring into the dark hollows where his eyes must be. "I beg for your help. It is a matter of life and death."

DuMort's expression didn't change, but his gaze shifted from my face to my neck. My neck, offering him a bouquet of purple petals. Voices floated around us like snowflakes: ice-cold and fleeting.

"She has no shame at all."

"What does one expect from someone like her? One can't rise above their station."

"Who lent the servant a dress?"

We were in a snow globe, DuMort and I, in a world of our own, entertainment to our observers.

A firm hand gripped my wrist and yanked at me. "This is a *private* gathering, as you have been told." This must be the Lady Wilcox, here to do what her husband dare not, and throw a pitiable woman onto the street.

I did not look back at the occultist as I was led away. He had heard my plea, had seen the severity of my case, and I had done irredeemable damage to my husband's name if anyone were to identify me. Now I had to go about gathering what remained of my dignity.

"One moment, please, Mrs Wilcox." DuMort's voice was deep and smooth, thrumming beneath the skin like the rumble of thunder. He rose from his seat then, and as he came around the table I saw that his fashion was strange. Unlike the stream-lined and slim men's suits around him, his outfit was made of black material that surrounded him neck-to-ankle in a voluminous gown. The gown seemed to move on its own, so that one could not say for certain whether that was the curve of his shoulder or a cut of the cloth, whether that was the bulge of his stomach or a billow of air. He was tall though, that much was certain, though not as tall as my husband, and his posture was greatly hunched, his ungloved hands fine and long-fingered. His eyes were as dark as mine, under heavy brows. His nose was narrow and slightly hooked, his cheek-bones sharp as a knife's edge. He was not what anyone would call handsome, but there was something that demanded rapt attention on a deeper level, in a way that made negligible flesh and bone and cartilage.

Mrs Wilcox gave me a look of pure hatred before she forced an indulgent smile onto her face. She turned to her guest of honour. "Yes?"

He approached us and lowered his voice. "I would be eter-nally grateful if you would allow this woman to stay for this evening. A special request of mine, if you will. This is some-thing I should like her to see."

The hostess tightened her grip on my wrist, but I would not give her the benefit of a reaction. She was much stronger than I, and her hand rough beneath the greasy cream she'd applied. "I do not want her here." The guests could surely hear the venom in her whispers, but they were stiff-backed and faking conversation around us.

"She will not speak, merely sit quietly and observe. I would be in your debt, and you would be helping a woman in need." Decency required me to remove myself from the situa-tion, thus dissolving their conflict, but I did not. Instead, I studied the watercolour on the far wall, as if they were not discussing me. A painted bird within a metal cage, singing despite its captivity.

This man might well be my last hope.

Mrs Wilcox must have been soulless. "Surely a lady of her standing could arrange to have you over to her own home?" she hissed. "We have planned this evening for months. The risk we have taken ..."

DuMort bowed deeply, his dark hair moving as he bent: the respectful motion was clipped and cold. "As you wish. I will accompany the lady home then. Have a wonderful evening."

The kind expression he wore on his face blunted his sharp features, and he held out his hand to me. "Miss?" Despite the scandalised murmurs of our audience, I reached out immediately to grasp it.

Chapter Two

We had not walked more than two steps before Mrs Wilcox simpered towards us. "Of course. Of course the woman may stay. You would disappoint so many people, Mr DuMort, if you left right now. So many other people in need, like your friend here."

Her face was contorted with rage, but she managed a demure curtsy. Her skirts slid against the floor like whispered insults, and her rough hands were clenched into fists amidst the rich cloth.

DuMort's expression exuded gratitude. He released me and turned to her. "You are a most generous woman, Mrs Wilcox." He bowed deeply over her hand, his lips almost grazing her knuckles. He wore a wedding ring on his right hand, unpolished and made from metal rather than wood.

He straightened up, and his bilious gown shifted with him. The shadows reached towards him like obsequious servants. Like seeping wet. "I am ready. Please gather your guests."

The hostess beamed at him and clapped her hands together.

"Master DuMort is about to start. Please, whoever wishes to speak with him, ready your offerings and take a seat at the table." She lost her smile when she looked at me, and jutted her chin towards one of the chairs against the wall. "You can sit in the corner."

He walked beside me towards his place, staring down at his toes, face pensive. His clothing hissed as he moved. At my questioning glance he looked at my assigned seat. "Watch me. Watch me well. And if, at the end of this night, what you see is palatable, I will do my best to help."

The chair the hostess indicated was behind DuMort's seat, far from the table, but I dared not complain. I sat down in the wooden chair and tried to still my shaking knees, to calm my frantic heart. I was bold; necessity had made me bolder than any other woman I knew, but true need made one vulnerable, dropped all defences. I felt as though I had crawled, unclothed, before Mrs Wilcox and DuMort to beg for aid. As though I were a helpless child again, at the mercy of flaxen-haired strangers.

But he had agreed to speak with me after the show. For whatever reason, he had shown me kindness, more kindness than anyone had for many years. I would see whatever the man wanted me to see, and then I would tell him of my sister's endless rage. Unlike the other occultists who crawled like vermin through this city, DuMort had genuine ability. Everyone said so. It was why he could not stay in any place for long: crowds began to follow him, and violence soon followed. He was a brave or greedy soul to even enter Mydalla, with our strange laws and brutal punishments.

The guests filled the room. Some took seats in the chairs that lined the walls, though none yet near me. Others rushed towards the single round table where the lone candle burned. There were long rectangular plates set in front of each seat, no more than four inches long and twice as wide. The sight of these wooden trays stopped some of the eager guests, and they retreated to the wall to join the onlookers.

I frowned. I had not considered payment, but was his cost so prohibitive? It was no matter. Whatever the amount, I would pay it.

Three people took seats at the table. The men reached into the pockets of their suit jackets, the sole woman her purse. I leaned forwards to see. The first young man laid a cord of brown thread across his tray. The other set down a vial of grey powder. The third, an old woman, tossed something small and white onto the table: it rattled on the rectangular plate like a die.

Another woman took the last seat. She wore a young woman's tight ringlets, but her face was lined, her movements stiff. She took a small, black parcel, no larger than her palm, from the man accompanying her. As she unwrapped it, a copper taste licked the back of my throat even through the colognes and perfumes in the air. The dark material hid it well, but I was sure I smelled blood.

Whatever was in her hand, whatever bled into the cloth, never reached my eyes. DuMort held out one of his elegant hands. "You may leave it covered." She nodded, and placed her small offering on the last empty tray.

The occultist looked at each of the guests at the table. "I will convey messages with their original intent. This may prove painful, but there is no use in arguing. The dead are stubborn, and often cruel. Take what information you can, as you will not have much time."

Some in the room reacted as DuMort spoke of things forbidden by the gods. Whether from lascivious pleasure or overwhelming fear, I saw suppressed shivers, bit lips, exchanged glances: they were, all of them, complicit this unholy night, a tryst between mortal and damned. No one looked at me, kept apart from the others even in our mutual desecration.

DuMort took from his voluminous robes a silk bag, dyed a blue so vivid it must have come from DongTian itself, and shook out its contents. Many small spheres of marked ivory clattered onto the tablecloth. This man knew something of the land from which my mother had fled. The land which had given me my blessed, cursed features, that ensured I could never belong here. DuMort bent his hunched form further towards the table and muttered in what sounded like DongTi, a tongue as lost to me as the warmth of my mother's arms.

It should have felt like a mockery. Somehow, with the utter seriousness of DuMort's expression and the fearful anticipation of the guests, it felt mystical. I, by proximity, became so as well.

DuMort bent this way and that, poring over his oracle spheres as if they held secrets. I'd seen others study polished crystal, or scattered tea leaves, in much the same manner. Fortunes were to be told first this night.

He sat before the ivory spheres, none larger than my thumbnail, and read from them. His voice did not ring out across the room like other performers I'd seen, but it reached those watching from the walls nonetheless. His voice rumbled low like an unfurling carpet, traversing upwards from our shoes, conducted through bone to sound in my mind. I shivered: he was at the table across the room, and yet directly behind me, lips murmuring against the shell of my ear. I leaned back, expecting to feel his warmth, but it was the cold parlour wall that kissed my shoulder blades instead.

Divinations are as meaningless to onlookers as condolences are to the dead. To the people these predictions are for, however, they can mend—or rend—hearts. Both happened at the round table this evening: wild, fierce reactions of joy or despair by people who somehow trusted this strange, unfamiliar man. I smoothed a lock of my hair, frowning. Wasn't I doing the same?

The spheres clattered faintly as DuMort gathered them back into the vivid blue bag with graceful movements. From this angle, his hooked nose and curved back looked more pronounced, a bird of prey hunched over offerings of food.

He sat then, hands beneath the table, dark eyes open but unfocused. When long moments passed without movement or sound, the people seated by the walls shuffled and whispered amongst each other. The lone candle flame at the round table stirred, whipping from its wax wick like it meant to lick the faces nearby.

DuMort spoke again. His voice was different, in cadence and pitch, but his expression did not change.

"Mother? Mother, it's Henry."

The first woman who sat at the table cried out and looked around as if she might have DuMort's sight. "Henry! Mummy's here." Her voice cracked as she spoke, and I turned away from her terrible grief.

"Mother. Please stop crying. Your tears disturb my peace. I could rest, if only you'd stop."

The old woman cried harder. "What of your da? Is he at peace? Did he find you?"

DuMort's face was blank, but the voice that came from his mouth was filled with confusion. "Da? ... I didn't know he'd ... I didn't know. Wherever I am, whatever *this* is. Da's not here."

The old woman clutched her head with two arthritic claws. Not a sound escaped her open mouth, only spittle.

A worm of doubt began to eat at my hope. This was not so different from the other performers I'd seen, those who enticed spirits to knock on tables or pretended to fall into trances. Those men peddled in grief, took money from the desperate, gave nothing but smoke and mirrors in return.

I shifted in my seat, wondering if this was what DuMort

wanted me to see: that he was no different than the other frauds. Or perhaps he thought I might be impressed with his oracles and his acting.

The show continued, but I could no longer stomach DuMort and his lies. I stood and walked across the room. No gentleman stood respectfully as I passed. No one acknowledged me at all.

My ripped cloak hung abandoned on the stair railing, and I took this proof of my folly with me. Before I reached the foyer, a large silhouette appeared in the front door's fogged glass. I stepped back into the parlor and pulled on Mrs Wilcox's sleeve like a frightened child.

She looked at me irritably before following my gaze. Her eyes widened and she turned to her guests, her whisper as loud as a yell. "The gendarmes! Run!"

Well-dressed gentry sprang from their seats with cries of panic and ran haphazardly like flies scattered from dung, shoving each other aside and to the floor, scrambling back to their feet, disappearing from the side and back doors into the cover of the cold night.

Mr Wilcox grabbed hold of DuMort and dragged him from the table. The payment trays, once holding an item in each, were empty. The two men whisked by me, and I, uncertain where to go, followed them.

"If they find an occultist in our house, both of us will be hanged," Mr Wilcox hissed as he dragged the taller man down to the wood-panelled cellar. "You mustn't be caught. If you are, do not name us, I beg of you. Our lives depend on it."

The cellar held a lamp, its flame set low, as if ready for this scenario. It smelled like damp earth, and a jumble of furniture and knickknacks were shoved into the corners where the lamplight didn't quite reach.

Wilcox pulled open a well-hidden door, its opening invisible amidst the vertical wall panels. The doorway was utterly dark, blacker than any natural night. DuMort nodded and plunged through the exit without hesitation, and he disappeared immediately. The void yawned wide again, waiting for me.

My long skirts tripped my tired feet as I crept up the wooden steps. "For mercy's sake, hurry!" expectorated Mr Wilcox, and he pushed me into the darkness himself.

Something wrapped around my face and arms, spiderwebs as thick as twine, and only the fear of their weaver kept my mouth from opening to scream. I pushed forward, frantic, arms flailing and catching at every step, and then I won free. Sight returned to me, and fresh air chilled the sweat on my skin and calmed my thumping heart. A creak of hinges behind me, and I turned back. Ivy clung thickly against the side of the house, hiding the doorway I had just passed through.

"Come on!" DuMort's voice whispered from the gloom, and I hurried to find him, afraid to be left alone. Following his dark, hunched form, we ran along the shadows behind the house. We crossed two, then three of the neighbours' yards, before hiding in the space between houses, the buildings so close together I felt trapped.

I crept closer to the street, leaning out to see the Wilcox's front door. And I was not the only one: people's shapes appeared in the windows of other houses, like the balcony seats of a theatre, watching the show.

The uniformed gendarmes emerged, holding the Wilcoxes in custody, and those guests that were too slow or defiant to run. Two silver-painted stagecoaches waited outside the house, their horses steaming and frothy-coated in the chill. The rhyme every citizen learns in their childhood ran through my head at the sight: *silver coaches for those who can't be saved/ The police fill jail cells while the gendarmes dig graves.*

My husband's carriage was parked further down the street, the driver looking around nonchalantly. I could walk a short distance to climb into the warmth of the coach and return home, back to my life. Untouched by all this, and the trouble that was sure to follow.

I looked behind me. DuMort remained unmoving in the shadows. The gendarmes crammed one stagecoach full of evil criminals who dared mourn loved ones. The officers fanned out, heads turning, truncheons in their hands. Someone had likely informed them that this was no amateur seance: their steps too determined, their eyes too keen. They knew an occultist had been present.

DuMort's voice, soft and deep as velvet, touched my ears. "You should go, Mina. They only want me."

Before I could ask him how he knew my name, there was a shout from the street. One of the officers barked an order, and boots clattered towards us. DuMort turned to run: back where we'd come, back where the darkness could hide him.

I looked again at the well-lit street and my husband's vehicle, touching cold-numbed fingers to my bruised throat.

Then I turned towards the darkness, picking up my skirts and following DuMort wherever he might lead, running as if the very hounds of hell were chasing me.

Chapter Three

We did not speak. Not when we emerged on an unfamiliar street, out of breath and limping, and not when we climbed into a rickshaw that DuMort managed to hail.

How quickly *he* and *I* became *we*. As fast as a guest-of-honour became a man on the run; as fast as a lady turned her back on the life she knew. As fast as infatuation might intoxicate a lonely soul.

I reminded myself of the disgust I'd felt for his performance this night, how heartlessly he'd mined grief for his own gain. Despite the deformity he aimed to hide with his costume, he had a strong charisma, and I would be wise to gird myself from its effects.

The roads were nearly empty at this time of night. We were lucky indeed to happen upon this driver, who pulled our combined weight with ease, whistling tunelessly as his strong legs powered us forwards. His features were similar to mine, but his skin lighter, and I knew what he assumed I must be when he saw me in my dishevelled state with a gentleman like DuMort.

The occultist sat close beside me in the narrow seat: the lines of our legs were pressed against each other, through his strange, thick garment. A faint scent of musk cologne teased my nose, momentary reprieves from the oil and smoke spit out by the street lanterns on this moist night. Our breaths steadied as we rested, but my sweat-slicked skin sprouted gooseflesh in the cold. I settled my broken cloak around my shoulders and burrowed into its warmth, daring no questions, not while the rickshaw driver was so close, nor the gendarmes still on alert.

DuMort cleared his throat. "Stop here, please." He passed some coin to the driver and turned to help me down. We were in an area of the city I never frequented, by the docks. It was a place for travellers and merchants, those who placed no roots and left no trace. There were more people about here, large men in rags who swayed on solid ground and reeked of spirits; well-dressed men with dreamy-looking eyes who smelt of flowers; officers on patrol who ignored us all.

He led me down one street and then another, close enough that I wrinkled my nose against the reek of brine and fish, close enough to hear the boats creak and knock against their moorings. Still I did not speak, afraid of drawing attention and unsure what to say. We stopped in front of a door that looked like the others, unlit and unmarked. DuMort rapped his knuckles against it, and a moment later a middle-aged woman greeted him, stepping aside to let us pass. Once her eyes travelled from the crown of my head to my scuffed boots, she ignored me entirely, something I was grateful for. I could not explain what I was doing with a strange man in his quarters without a chaperone: not to myself, and certainly not to any other.

I followed him up two narrow flights of stairs. My boots had become expensive torture devices, and a fluid thicker than sweat squelched between boot and foot with each step. I pulled myself up using the banister with one hand, the other holding my ruined skirts.

His rented apartments were larger than I expected. He took the lantern that hung outside his door and went from lamp to lamp, lighting each until the rooms were filled with a cheery yellow glow. Beyond the foyer, there was a small kitchen to the left, and two doors, the furthest of which he gently closed. Only then did he speak, taking my arm and assisting me to the small dining table and two chairs set nearby. "My wife is unwell," he said. "You must not disturb her."

It was the way in which he placed the responsibility upon me, the woman he had brought into his wife's apartment, that raised my ire—how quickly again does *we* become *you*—but I had more important things to discuss.

"You said you would help me." I sat down quickly to take the weight from my feet, and near groaned with relief. "I have money."

"That is one of the payments, yes." DuMort's deep-set eyes were pools of shadows across from me: from this angle, they looked like empty sockets, his sharp features a skull.

I recalled the rectangular trays. "And the other?"

He reached into one pocket and then another, placing objects onto the table like a magician. The vial of powder, the plaited threads, the dark-wrapped parcel. The small item that sounded like a die as it hit the tray. I peered closer in disbelief: it was a molar.

"Coin is useless for the dead," DuMort said softly, and the expression on his face was a mystery. "Instead, I require a sacrifice to weed out the frivolous, and the only thing that will satisfy any spirit: a gift of flesh."

His words might have been part of a spell, for as he spoke them my vision cleared. It was not a vial of powder on the table, but ash. The plait of thread was human hair. And the parcel whose black wrapping was stiff with dried blood ... I looked at the closed door. "Does your wife know that you collect these grim wares? What happens to these painfully parted gifts?" And yet I did not leave. I did not even pretend to consider leaving. Truth be told, I wasn't sure how I might return to the safety of my home.

"I dispose of them," DuMort answered.

"You toss these remnants of loved ones aside like garbage? Or is there a ritual?" I felt a fraud, asking these questions, as if I were considering such a thing.

"A ritual. Yes, that is an appropriate term. I offer these payments to appease the spirits, to ensure my conduit will answer the next time I call. You will have to find something like these for me."

Silence fell over both of us like a gossamer web, growing thicker and heavier with each guttering of the lamps. There were words to break the tension, words I could not say, and the silence deepened, until I was as voiceless and helpless as the sad remains before me.

DuMort clucked his tongue. "Ah. I did not imagine you to be squeamish."

"It's not that," I said, bristling. "Well, it's not only that."

"What is it then?"

"It's ... it's ... *selfish*." Heat flooded my cheeks, though I was unsure whether it was embarrassment or anger. "To violate the vessels of those who have passed on, just for a few answers. Once someone has passed, they are elevated. They are saints. It's wrong to defile such holy remains."

The occultist pressed a hand over his sternum as if my words caused him pain. "It's late, and that is a discussion for another time, if you wish. These are my terms, and you may decide whether or not you accept them."

A desperation rose in me at the dismissal in his tone. I thought of all that I'd risked and endured for this moment, the vengeful spirit that awaited my return. I gestured to the bruises on my throat. "My life is in danger. Please do not turn me away. There must be something, anything else, I might provide in exchange."

He leaned closer to me, dispelling the shadows that settled within the contours of his face. Death became a man once more. His gaze lingered on my face and throat, appraisingly, and I bit back the urge to set conditions on my offer. We were both married, after all. Once again, I stayed quiet. I did not wish to insult him by presuming.

Finally he nodded, leaning back against his chair where the shadows claimed him once more. "I am in need of an assistant while in Mydalla," he said. "Mine refused to set foot in this town, whose rigid laws require us to scuttle about like criminals."

"An assistant?" I gave a small laugh of relief. "That's easily managed. Our house has many qualified servants. You may have your choice, as long as you treat them well."

"You misunderstand me. I require an assistant for my shows. Someone who will not be cowed by the rich. Someone who will lend my DongTi occultism some credibility."

I stared at him, not understanding.

"I want *you*, Mina." His voice thrummed deep, and despite the warning I'd given myself on the rickshaw, my heart beat faster as a part of me passed his lips.

"How did you know my name?" I asked, suspicion overcoming the thrill. I should have asked earlier. It seemed far too coincidental that he had promised to help me, and brought me to his apartment, just as he was seeking a DongTi assistant.

He made a graceful, dismissive gesture. "There will be time for questions later. I want only one, important answer. Will you join me?"

I was no stranger to work. Before my mother had died and I'd been adopted by Lady Summerhill, I'd helped my mother with all the chores. As a noblewoman, I was excellent with needle and thread, and danced quite well. But it was not as simple as whether or not I could perform the tasks of an assistant: I would be recognised now, subject to speculation as to why a woman of means such as myself would tie herself to such illicit labour. Edgar would no doubt be humiliated, his good name dragged down by his common wife, the way his friends had warned so many years ago.

My eyes rested again on his wife's closed door. Despite his hunched figure and questionable acts, I felt a powerful pull towards this man, an attraction I'd never felt before. For that reason alone I should refuse, out of loyalty to my husband and my own virtue.

Yet what was the alternative? I had come all this way, and might not survive my sister's next nocturnal visit. Someone had to intervene, and there was no one I could speak to about her death. Not in Mydalla, and the other occultists I'd consulted were worse than useless. DuMort knew of my culture, had been to the home I'd never seen with adult eyes: there were things I could learn from him, and in doing so, I might better remember my culture, my mother.

"I will join you," I answered firmly, to chase away my lingering doubts. The lantern closest to us hissed and flared, brightening the room like a tiny sun.

DuMort looked at the light with wide eyes until it faded back to dimness. "Tis a deal that pleases the spirits." He himself did not look pleased: instead, his features were tight with tension, his shoulders stiff and near his ears.

We clasped hands to cement our deal, his strong hand devouring mine, the shifting flame our only witness.

Or so I thought.

Chapter Four

Edgar stirred when I slipped into bed, though I left only a slit in my lantern to light my way. As if I were a thief hiding in darkness rather than a lady in her own home.

"Where have you been?" he muttered, his voice thick with sleep and irritation.

"I'll tell you tomorrow," I said. He would not press me for answers: his heart was not in it. Had not been in it for many years. I slid into the warmth of the bed and gingerly slipped my newly washed feet beneath the heavy covers. My boots' embroidery was ruined, stained scarlet and brown, and I did not wish the same fate for my sheets.

My husband grunted in response. His breathing deepened a moment later, and I was left alone again. I shut the lantern on my nightstand and tried to make peace with the night's events.

After we had come to our agreement, DuMort had woken his driver, staying nearby. Though he must have been as exhausted as I, the occultist rode with me to the familiar balustrades of the Braithwaite estate house, and did not depart until a yawning manservant opened my front door.

In the safety of my home, chasing sleep, I did not wish to dwell on the ride home, on the feeling that rode in the carriage with us, full of things that could not be said. I was near-bursting with the energy I'd felt between us: surely he felt the same, though he'd said little. It was an utterly different quiet from the one between Edgar and I, which was as empty as the nursery. Or perhaps that was a difference I wished to see, and it was my delusion that painted awkwardness romantic, and comfortable silence resentful.

I could not think of those long moments, no, nor of the sharp-edged bones that stood out in DuMort's face like chiaroscuro: my heart kept skipping, light as a young girl's feet. I turned my head to stare at the comfortable lines of Edgar, lines that had softened with age and comfort, and tried to stir up a sense of loyalty to the man brave enough to marry me.

Only resentment, ever banked, flared at the effort. Edgar was a clear pane of glass compared to the occultist's shroud of mystery. He had spoken to his driver outside while I sat warm in the carriage, and so I only heard DuMort's parting words as he clambered in. "I thought it was Society Men. Imagine being relieved they were only gendarmes."

He was braver than those who resided within Mydalla's walls. The priests and gendarmes worked together like handle and scythe blade, keeping us on our knees lest we lose our heads. I had survived something I never thought possible, had fled the scene of the crime with the perpetrator himself. I would be a part of future acts.

Sleep was a flickering will-o'-wisp I could not catch, though I fatigued in the chase. The shade of my sister appeared in the corner where the deepest shadows gathered, only recognisable by the malevolence emanating from her dark silhouette. I was grateful I could not see her face, her once-willowy body, contorted with her hatred for me.

We stared at each other as the silver moonlight seeped through the shuttered windows, sending slats of light across the rug on the floor. When we were young, staring into each other's faces in our shared bed, SuChin would ease me into slumber by singing with her sweet voice. As a spirit, she was silent as she waited for sleep to claim me: I stayed alert, my cotton nightgown clinging to my sweat-lined skin, but I remained powerless against her. I had no defence against spirits: no talisman, potion, or prayer had ever worked, save for my awareness. As long as I could see her, she had not yet come close, satisfying herself with knocking over a knickknack or two in retaliation. It was when my eyelids grew heavy as anchors, and sleep was a riptide pulling me under the cold depths—then she grew brave, pulling at my hair or scratching me, or sitting astride my chest to wrap strong fingers around my neck.

We looked at each other for eternity, and never did my fear wane, nor my heart slow, though I had known this shade for years. Only when dawn came, the pink rays stripping the layers of darkness from the corners until she had no cover, and she faded away with the last of the night, did my breathing steady, my sweat dry. I'd seen her in the daylight, but rarely; like the unholy creatures in storybooks, her presence was stronger in darkness, as if she fed off shadows.

The maids knocked to bring us tea and set up our clothing. Edgar changed quickly and sat at his customary seat by the balcony. I gazed outwards at the awakening city, at the crematorium's tall spires, billowing smoke and the spirits of the dead heavenwards. Were the priests right? Did the living doom freed souls by speaking of them—were angels dragged down by their wings, saints ripped from the safety of the clouds just by calling their names? The streets filled with carriages and horses, their distant noises reaching our balcony from across our neatly-groomed estate, while I waited for my husband's questions about last night. Edgar sipped at his weak tea and read his newspaper as usual, and uttered nought a word.

I added milk and sugar to my cup, and took a breath. "I will be assisting a visitor in his work for several weeks."

"Oh? Who is the visitor?" My husband's voice came from behind his raised newspaper.

I lowered my voice so no one would overhear. I had considered lying, for Edgar was the type to follow every law—of course he would, for the laws were made to benefit those like him—but I owed him honesty, if not love.

"It is the famed occultist, Alexandre DuMort." I tried to keep my voice as bland as my husband's tea.

The newspaper snapped downwards. Edgar's expression was neutral, but his tone was firm. "As your husband, I cannot allow you to associate with an infamous criminal."

"You are my husband, not my master. He promises to help me with my sister's ghost."

Edgar snorted as his cheeks grew mottled. "You don't need an occultist. You need an asylum."

I pushed from my chair to approach his, and leaned over him, tilting my head so his eyes were in line with my neck. "And these bruises? Who do you think hurts me, if this is all in my mind?"

Instead of a response, his hand reached out to take mine. I had once loved his touch, as infrequent as it was gentle. My ire softened at this unexpected show of tenderness, until he placed my own fingertips against the fading bruises on my neck.

His voice held nothing, not even sadness, as he withdrew from me again. "A perfect match."

Once we had faced the world together. I was sure of it. I wouldn't have married him otherwise. I was stronger as a young woman. "You don't control me, Edgar. I told you as a courtesy, not for permission."

I turned to look back at him before I left our bedroom, but he had raised his newspaper once more, the coarse pages as impenetrable as stone.

~

I RETURNED to the address DuMort had given me, my eyes now able to see the small discreet mark on doors that were otherwise identical. The same woman let me in, her blue-eyed gaze looking past me as if I weren't there. As if I were nothing. It was a look I was well-familiar with.

The daylight made clear the uneven steps, the cracks in the walls, the insects that skittered at my approach. Others said that DuMort regularly performed for nobles and kings. Why demean himself to come to Mydalla?

I knocked on his apartment, the small sips of tea churning in my stomach. Perhaps the attraction I'd felt for him last night was a figment of my imagination, sparked by his forbidden renown, further enflamed by the chase from the gendarmes. Part of me hoped this was the case: that I was loyal, heart and soul, to Edgar, as I had vowed before the priests, but another part of me was fearful that such a powerful chemistry could be wrong.

DuMort opened the door, and my churning stomach tightened at the sight of him. I looked at the man in proper, steady light for the first time: dark eyes framed by long lashes, a heavy brow, his nose and cheekbones as sharp as the razor he'd slid against his jaw this morning. His lips were thin, his forehead high, and his jaw tapered. I searched for some sign of DongTian in his features, some explanation of his use of eastern magicks, but I found none.

His eyes crinkled, and I flushed at my scrutiny. "My sister's ghost came to visit me last night," I said as I entered his apartment and sat on the same chair I'd occupied a few hours ago. "Will you ask her why she will not leave me be?"

DuMort closed the door gently behind me—automatically my eyes checked his wife's door, still closed—and went to the small wood stove where he was boiling water. It surprised me to see a man of his stature performing so mundane a task, but I suppose he had no choice with an ill wife and no assistant. Today he wore black pants that fit snug around long legs, similar to Mydallan fashion, but his shirt reached halfway down his thighs, a billowing dark cloud that floated around his body, ever-shifting. A thin, silver chain hung from his neck, the rest of the necklace hidden in his shirt.

"We have an engagement tonight, you and I," he said in response. "We must use the little time we have to prepare you. It is my wish that you learn these practices well enough to perform them yourself."

"Surely we have a few minutes," I protested.

"It is difficult to speak to the dead more than once a day, but I can try after the performance." DuMort set tea and buns between us. "This is one of the first things you must learn, to help me conserve my energy. To channel, one requires a conduit, a ... translator, if you will, that can decipher the messages."

"And how do you find this conduit?" I placed my silk gloves on my lap to pick up a bun: it was warm and soft to the touch, with a sweetness in the dough. Somehow, though he was a visitor here, DuMort had found a DongTi baker.

"It isn't easy," he grimaced. "But once you have one, a loyal one, the impossible becomes as easy as reading a newspaper."

I thought of Edgar on the balcony, hiding behind his wall of newsprint, and I wondered if somehow DuMort had plucked the image from my mind.

"If you can hear the spirits, why bother with tools?" I asked. "You had oracles in a blue bag."

He unfolded his slender limbs from his seat and went to his large cloak, pulling from one of its unseen pockets the dyed bag I'd seen the night before. "The conduit hears the spirits, yes. But it is a tiresome process. Tools help the dead communicate more easily. We use these for fortune-telling." He spilled the contents of the bag into his cupped palm and held them out to me.

Upon closer inspection, the yellow- and grey-stained oracles weren't spherical: they were more like smoothed cubes, and engraved with mystical symbols, painted red or black, on four sides. The other two ends were ground smooth. It wasn't until I had picked one up and recognised the familiar ridges that I understood what I held, and hurriedly put the molar back into his hand, wiping my fingers on my velvet skirts.

"An occultist trades in *human* flesh and spirit," DuMort told me. "His instruments must be made of the same." He poured his oracles back into the bag, the teeth chattering against each other. "That's one of the ways you can find a fraud. You cannot trust one who uses mechanical devices or animal sinew to speak to the dead."

We returned to our seats to finish the lesson. The sonorous voice of Alexandre—for that is what he insisted I call him—accompanied my meal. My mouth nibbled the sweet buns and sipped strong, dark tea while my other senses hungered for the man himself, though only one appetite could be sated. I tried —gods, how I tried!—to maintain an aloofness between us, but no barrier could protect me from the light of his charm. My earlier reservations fell away like falling petals, leaving my core exposed and basking in the warmth of Alexandre's sun.

Time passed in an instant, though that was always the way of pleasant things. Alexandre stood up and helped me to the door.

"I will send my carriage to your home at dusk."

"What should I wear?" I asked. It was a silly thing to ask of a man, but I had no choice.

He bowed as I left, the uneven curve of his back growing more pronounced as he did. "Wear whatever you think appropriate to confer with the dead," he said. "I trust your judgment."

During the short walk to his driver, I pulled the cowl of my wool cloak over my face to hide my flushed cheeks. What a foolish question to ask when one planned to break the city's oldest law.

I should wear the scarlet stripes of convicted criminals, or the sickly yellow of women committed to asylums. Would my sister's ghost find me even there? Would imprisoning my body free me from her rage?

I lifted my chin and squared my hunched shoulders. I would risk it, if it meant freedom from my tormentor.

Another thought flitted through my mind, the only place I might be honest.

I *would* risk it all.

Everything I owned.

To spend more time with him.

Chapter Five

I sat beside Edgar for dinner, but we did not share the meal. Sharing requires some sense of intimacy, but we were not at the table together. The only words we uttered were meant for the servants, the air, anything but each other.

I did not taste the food. I may as well have swallowed Alexandre's bag of molars: it pierced my gullet, gnawed my stomach, twisted my guts. My plate remained untouched. My eyes travelled over my husband's features, the way they'd traversed Alexandre's a few hours earlier.

Edgar's once-pleasant face had grown aloof and unhandsome over the decade we had been married: I am sure he felt the same about mine. Falling in love colours the cheeks and brightens the eyes, primes lips to smile or kiss. We were once flowers, now dried into husks; we were marble busts, crumbling into dust.

Eva, one of the maids, came to announce a carriage had arrived. Edgar stood as I departed—but he said nothing, and his eyes never left his plate.

Night fell quickly in the waning season. The lamps lit above our doorway blazed bright, stealing my night vision as I passed. So it was that I gave no more than a polite greeting to the figure who waited at the coach steps, until I heard his voice.

"You look beautiful, Mina." Alexandre had come to get me himself.

I did not trust my voice to answer, not just yet. So I settled myself inside the carriage and smoothed my dark skirts. I knew what might happen at these performances now: any secret might be spilled, and any life with it. My shoes were slippers, as easy to run in as my own bare feet, and I had chosen a soft cotton dress that moved quietly, without the stiffness of corset or the bulk of crinoline. Alexandre climbed in after me, his strange bulbous gown constantly shifting, even when he was still.

My smile was small, though his words filled me with great joy. I was afraid of cracking the layers of make-up on my face. I had taken my mother's things from her trunk, decades old. The face powder was clumsily applied, stiff and patchy; the circles of pink were unevenly placed, the red lacquer lips garish as blood. I had never learned the DongTi way; had relied on my fading memories of my mother getting ready for parties, as proud as I was ashamed, accentuating her distinctive features even as I learned to hide mine. My sister would have remembered. I clung to a faded memory of her painting my face when we were children, her hands gentle and sure, until our mother chased us away from her make-up. She'd been six years older than me; her boldness and quick smile had drawn everyone's eyes. I'd once hidden in her shadow: now, her ghost hunted me from mine.

Tonight, I was hiding again. I hid behind Alexandre's presence, behind the thick, unfamiliar mask of my ancestors. It was to protect Edgar's reputation, I reminded myself, whenever my cowardice grew intolerable. Alexandre would leave in a few weeks, and the damage I helped him wreak would remain mine and Edgar's alone.

The streets grew narrower and older, the cobblestone roads rougher. I looked at the small, squat structures, and remembered a time I considered them palaces.

"I prefer to lend my gifts to those with less," Alexandre murmured.

"More easily tricked?" I asked without thinking.

He tsked at me, but his tone was mild. "So many of the rich are cynics. Those who carry less money carry more faith. In gods, in their loved ones, in a better life after this." He looked out the window, the hook of his nose both elegant and fierce. "They are easier to help."

He knocked on the stagecoach's wall and the driver pulled the horses to a stop. I was glad of it: my jaw was stiff from keeping my teeth from rattling, and my rump ached from the many bumps and jolts.

We walked through a small street, the air full of coarse smoke and cooking odours. There were few carriages here, and none of the gendarmes' silver-painted ones. "How do you know it's safe?" I asked him. "That it's not some trick?"

Alexandre shrugged—his shoulders seemed to move, anyway, though I could not be sure. "I, too, must trust in a power beyond myself."

The house he took us to stood in near shambles. Paint peeled from the rotting wood around the frame, and rather than glass or fresh silk, rough burlap covered each window. He knocked, gently, but the door was so water-damaged it barely made a sound.

He cleared his throat and called out. "I'm looking for Miss Tessa."

Shushing louder than any whispers met his words, and a pang of concern struck me, which solidified when I saw the young waif who opened the door.

"Who are you?" she asked, her eyes darting between the both of us. A smaller boy, his jaw thrust out belligerently, stood just behind her, an unsprouted guardian wearing clothes far too large on him, fastened with twine.

Alexandre gave his courtly bow, not one fraction shallower than he gave wealthy Mrs Wilcox the night before. "I am the occultist DuMort, and this is my assistant Mina."

The girl, for she could not yet be eighteen, relaxed her bony shoulders to let us in, reassuring the boy with a gentle cupping of his head.

There was only one main room, with threadbare blankets folded in one corner near the wood stove. Adults huddled within, better dressed and better fed than the two children, waiting for Tessa's nod to step forwards and greet us. Alexandre emptied his numerous hidden pockets and handed me the items I'd learned about earlier. I placed them on a rickety table, guarding them, but no one had eyes for anyone but him.

The night passed in a blur of nerves: I wanted to do my job well; I was nervous the opaque burlap sacks that covered the windows hid approaching gendarmes; I wanted only good news for Tessa and her siblings. Aside from the young boy, there were two other girls, younger still. Their faces were scrubbed but their calloused hands were stained with dirt not so easily cleaned. I rubbed my hands together at idle moments, my silk gloves removed and stored in a skirt pocket: it was years ago, and yet only yesterday, that my palms were thickened, rough calluses growing over blood blisters and oily grime like pale barnacles.

There were not enough chairs. Alexandre sat on the floor, gestured for the others to do the same. I collected the flesh payments from the trays: dried umbilical cord coiled like a snail, a swath of leathery skin, a wooden cup of clotted blood. The fourth offering was fresh—the tip of a thin finger, a tiny, perfect nail—and the silent boy with Tessa kneeled before the occultist, holding his bandaged hand in his lap.

DuMort transformed into a different man when he performed: his expressions more dramatic, his gestures extravagant and accentuated with flourishes. At his coaxing, I brought him his blue bag of engraved teeth, from which he told fortunes. The copper bowl with its powder mixture and wood chips was next: he hadn't used it last night. When the wood in the bowl was lit, the smoke acted strangely, changing colours and shifting before our very eyes. DuMort studied these sinuous forms carefully, his dark eyes piercing. "This house has a loving, gentle spirit within it. You will know its presence by the smell of flowers, or when words of a song appear in your mind."

"That's Mama," one of Tessa's little sisters cried out, and I looked away from the unfathomable yearning in the child's eyes. The void never shrank, I wanted to tell her, but she would one day grow around it.

DuMort frowned at the burning copper pot. "There is a second spirit here. Angry and jealous. He causes the thumping footsteps, and the foul smells. When he is here, his energy overpowers the other spirit."

"Can you get rid of that one?" the little boy asked, clutching hard at his bandaged finger. "Tell him to leave and never come back?"

"That is beyond what an occultist can do," DuMort told him kindly. "But for your sakes, I will try to send him the message."

DuMort bent his head, forehead creased with effort, and grunted. His floating gown seemed to puff out with power, and then deflated to fall flat against him once more. "Begone, Arnold," he commanded. "You are not welcome here any longer." The red fire, pulsing with dark blue, began to hiss.

The fire shifted rapidly, hues blending or standing out as if the flames themselves battled. Utter silence filled the room: people stood frozen, unblinking and unbreathing. I had never seen such magic, not from any occultist, and I wondered if this too were a trick Alexandre had brought back from DongTian. A plume of fire exploded upwards with a *fwoomp*. It filled the room with acrid smoke and then disappeared. People exclaimed with surprise, some with fear.

"Did it work?" the boy asked, his breathing ragged.

"Peter, look!" his younger sister shouted. "The fire!"

A small glow came from the copper bowl. The embers burned within, green as the leaves of a jade plant.

"That's her favourite colour." Tessa knelt beside her brother and hugged him tight against her.

"She will remain here, with you all. She sends her love," DuMort told them, his eyes shining. I wondered that the spirit did not speak through him the way I'd seen before. He clapped his hands together and turned to the others, who knelt in front of the offering trays. "Let's move on."

The rest of the messages were meaningless in comparison, at least to me. Fantasies once forbidden stretched before me, suddenly within reach: To speak to my sister, who wanted me dead; my father, who I couldn't remember; my mother, who I couldn't forget.

And then it was time to go. DuMort shook hands and murmured comforts as we left, the guests eager to touch him, as if it might confer blessings. I handed him his tools, and they disappeared once more into his gown.

I carried the copper bowl with its charred remains in my hand, and DuMort made some show of taking the worn bag of coins Tessa handed him. At the door, however, the occultist stumbled, landing hard against the smoke-yellowed wall.

The guests gasped. Some reached to help, and others drew back, perhaps afraid of angering the spirits. I waved them away and bent over him.

"Are you alright?" I asked, concern cracking through my thick make-up.

He looked dazed, unfocused. He nodded, and reached his hand out towards me. I mustered all the strength I could and pulled. DuMort stood up bonelessly, a marionette with invisible strings, and I knew then that his fall had been a dramatic ruse. To what end, I couldn't fathom.

"What do you need?" I said, my voice strained with the lie.

"A support, nothing more." DuMort gestured to Tessa's brother. "As man of the house, I must impose upon you for help, Master Peter."

He placed a large hand on the frail boy's shoulder, and slowly they walked out the door, towards our waiting carriage. I followed along behind them, bemused, and was about to throw the charred contents of the copper bowl onto the broken road, but DuMort stopped me.

"Save that, if you please. The ingredients are most hard to come by."

I nodded and righted the bowl once again, unsure how he had known my intentions. We stopped at the carriage door, and DuMort handed Peter the same bag Tessa had given him for payment. "Hide it well, young man. You understand?"

Peter's eyes widened, and he took the bag, secreting it under his overlarge shirt.

"Mind you move slowly, or your neighbours will hear the clinking."

The driver helped us both into the coach, and then we were jostling back towards the city centre once more.

"You didn't take the payment," I said.

Alexandre—for he'd shed his DuMort persona as quickly as one would a cloak—nodded. "What you witnessed tonight is something that only happens in Mydalla." He shook his head in a curt, angry movement. "These areas find the most desperate people to host these events. Often they are widows, or children. If the gendarmes were to come, the adults flee and leave the host to your law's savage mercies."

"That was clear to me." I was no stranger to desperate people doing desperate things, but I was moved by his rare act. "But you didn't take the payment, and for that you have lost a night's wages. I would like to replace what you lost."

Alexandre reached out to pat my hands resting atop my crossed legs. An unseen spark passed between us at his touch, making my heart leap and my core tighten. "You are kind, Mina. I thank you, but I can survive losing one night's coin." He looked out the window, his voice turning grim. "If only I could refuse all the payments we took from them tonight."

There were many more questions I wanted to ask, but his mood had changed. I mulled over his last words, and his previous claim that the flesh payments were offered to appease the spirits.

The way he said it—the expression on his face—I understood that if he did not continue to offer these human remains to the spirits, there would be dire consequences.

Chapter Six

"Mina. Are you alright?" The concern in Alexandre's voice softened the steel in my spine. It should have been my husband who spoke to me this way, who acknowledged the gouges on my face. Edgar had not even noticed what my sister's shade had done to me last night. I forced him to see, but he only muttered advice about seeking a poultice from an apothecary, and then I ceased once more to exist.

Alexandre tilted my chin upwards with gentle fingers and studied my injury, still seeping pink tears. Oh, the tenderness of his touch: I was dying of thirst and he offered me a sip of water. It would not save me, would merely soothe my bone-dry throat, make me realise how miserably parched I'd become. Still, I couldn't help but close my eyes at the sensation of another person touching me with such care, and my exhale shook with pent-up emotion.

Mina Braithwaite never cried in front of another person. Not when her mother died, leaving her alone in the world; not when she gave up the hope of having children; and certainly not now, at the merest kindness from a stranger.

I pulled away and spoke firmly. "Now will you please

speak to my sister's ghost? Or would you like to wait until I've joined her?" He'd begged off channelling for me the previous night, saying he was too drained. And so I suffered once more.

He shook his head, eyes still on my injuries. "This is not your sister's doing."

"How do you know?" I asked. "Have you seen her near me?" I lowered my voice. "Have you ... *spoken* to her?"

Alexandre's eyes widened, and he was silent a moment before answering. "A spirit wouldn't harm their own sister. It is unfathomable, unless there were reason for her fury." He hesitated. "We have an event tonight, as you know, but your safety is more important."

He sat me down on my usual wooden chair at the table. "How is your wife?" I asked, to make up for my cold manner. "I can send a physician over, if you'd like?"

I could not read the expression on his face. "It is not a condition that will improve. All I can do is keep her as comfortable as I can. Now, let us begin."

He bent his head, and his voice murmured DongTi prayers, words far beyond what I remembered.

"How did you learn to speak the language?" I asked.

"I lived there for many years, to study with their occultists. They know so much more than our Western practitioners." A moment of silence. "It was there I met my wife."

Ah. The admission evoked a tangled thread of emotions within me. He had agreed to help me not because my plight had moved him, but because I was his wife's countryman. Perhaps his eye had grown fond of DongTi features, and he wished to collect us. If he had married a DongTi woman, perhaps he found me attractive as well, and the fiery alchemy I'd felt between us was real.

There was silence in the apartments, save for my too-loud breathing and my beating heart. Alexandre was a statue carved from golden-hued wood, fading sunlight from the nearby window streaming over the left side of his face like a caress.

Our eyes met. I knew I should look down, but a wildness took hold of me and I held his gaze the way I wanted to hold his hand. The crackling energy I'd felt before passed between us again. It was nothing of the occult: it was the buzz of attraction, the heat of kindred souls. An energy I'd once had with Edgar.

He broke first, looking over my shoulder. His eyebrows drew close together as he frowned at what he saw.

"Why do you believe it is your sister who haunts you?" he asked.

"You mentioned a spirit needing a reason. She's angry with me." It was not easy to say the words, hard knots of guilt and shame unravelling from my chest like a pearl necklace. "Rightfully so. Our old house had a ..." I had never learned the word for it, not with Mydalla's strict laws, and had only heard my mother say it in DongTi. "... XieLin?"

"Evil spirit," he translated.

"It killed my father in his sleep. My mother took the last of our money and bought us passage here. Only SuChin ... she did not want to leave the house where our father died. She was sure his spirit remained, and he would be lonely. So she jumped off the boat as it pulled away, and the captain refused to turn back." I swallowed hard, the sight of my sister's shrinking form as the stinking barge drifted away. "My mother ... she was determined to save one of us, at least. And we left her. We left my sister behind. She was only thirteen. A few years ago, months after I learned of her death, SuChin began to haunt me."

"What do you think she wants?"

I spread my hands. "Revenge. For taking Mother away. For dooming her to a short, wretched life."

Alexandre stared beyond me, his focus so fixed I felt the urge to look over my shoulder as well.

I waited for him to assume a child's voice, or to speak her words for my hearing. Instead, he leapt to his feet, his chair legs growling across the floor. Alexandre strode behind me, waving his hands as if wafting away a putrid odour. He scowled as he returned to his place, but he didn't sit down again.

"What is it? What did SuChin say?" I had never seen him so agitated, though I'd only known him a matter of days.

He shook his head, refusing to look at me. "Nothing I understood."

"Maybe it's something that will only make sense to me," I urged. "She was my sister, after all."

Alexandre pressed his hands on the table surface as if the wood lent him strength. His loose shirt rustled around him, though he himself made no further movement. He was a trembling aspen with leaves of black, shaking in the windless room. Something had upset him.

"We must get ready," he said, instead of answering me. "The house we will visit is in your neighbourhood, in case you wish to dress accordingly."

Something about the guarded expression on his face shrivelled the questions on my tongue. As his driver took me back to the Braithwaite estate, the first hint of resentment bubbled within me: this was hardly a fair deal we had struck. I was working day and night with him, and in exchange I received nothing but grim looks and non-answers.

That wasn't all I gained from Alexandre, though I was loathe to admit it: We were both married to other people, after all, and he would leave within weeks. Even now, having just left him, I missed him like he was a part of me, some vital limb that made my heart light and my thighs heavy, that made me feel alive even as we worked with the dead. I felt haunted by the occultist. I yearned for him to slide into my orifices, to become one with me, body and soul. So that I might never feel lonely again.

Chill air cooled the heat in my cheeks and broke me from my reverie. The driver waited patiently, looking away from my scratched face, and beyond the open door I could see we had reached Edgar's house.

A few hours remained before the event, and I spent that time bathing, where the hot water might explain my blush and where I might pretend the scented oils gliding over every part of my naked body were Alexandre's long-fingered hands.

Mydalla was a forbidding land for its citizens: not only for its laws, but for its expectations. Women did not have appetites. We were expected to eat little and speak even less. Courtships and marriages held all the passion of business transactions, as emotionless as a scientist cross-pollinating different strains of peas. Once, I thought Edgar and I lucky, because we laughed and lusted and made love when the mood struck us. Over time, the laughter and lust faded, and our bed was used for nothing more than sleep and wistful tears. Though my appetite didn't lessen, our marriage withered. I believed, like the pea plants, that our season had passed. All that remained of our passion were desiccated stalks. Though I lived in a house full of servants and my husband, none would treat me as their friend.

I was as alone as I had been as an orphaned little girl.

I felt hope budding within me now, the first curls of life springing from the darkness and seeking the smallest ray of light. Futile and temporary though our arrangement might be, I felt something for Alexandre. Feeling anything at all reminded me I was, in fact, alive, not some steam-powered automaton awakening each day until the day I didn't. He might be the next man to fill the emptiness inside me.

When the bathwater turned cold and day turned to dusk, I

clambered out to prepare. The wounds on my face, scratches from SuChin, would fester under the old, thick make-up I'd worn before. Instead, I tried on a masquerade mask, turning my face this way and that. Only close friends might recognise me, and I had none of those.

I ate dinner beside Edgar. It felt as though I were seeing us for the first time. *He looks at his food, or around the room, but never at me.* We'd once giggled through meals, feeding each other some morsel or other from our plates, even though they held the same food. If one could fall in love, somehow we'd climbed out of it, and it felt like a death.

Alexandre's carriage arrived. I placed my silverware neatly and stood up. Edgar opened his mouth, and I waited, but it was only to take in another forkful of food. I strode through his house and down his walkway, wondering how many more small neglects would break a heart—would end a marriage.

Alexandre waited by the open coach, his sharp-edged face easing into a smile once he saw me. Leaving my husband's absent presence to be greeted so by another man: it felt sinful.

It felt wonderful.

As if I'd broken into a home in the chill winter night and found warmth in another's bed. It was neither the fault of the cold, nor the bed, but my heart only cared for comfort.

Alexandre leaned close to me from the other bench as we drove towards the event. "This may prove a challenging night for both of us," he warned. "If people ask you questions, only smile mysteriously and do not answer. If they believe you unable to speak Mydallan, so much the better."

"Who are they?" I asked.

He leaned back, and his voluminous gown deflated with his sigh. "Those who seek to discredit me, for reasons of their own."

"Is it the Society Men?" I asked.

Alexandre's eyes narrowed. "What do you know of them?"

"You mentioned them to your driver, that first night. That you were glad it was only the gendarmes."

His face lost its suspicion. "Ah. Yes, them."

"And they will be present tonight? How do you know?"

He gestured vaguely to the air. "The spirits hear many things, save what is kept safe in one's heart."

I considered the idea that with Alexandre, I was never truly alone, that a whisper spoken aloud might reach his ears. It felt intimate, as if we were connected no matter the distance.

"Will you tell me what you saw, earlier today?" I asked him after we'd ridden some time in silence.

"Mina." He took both of my hands in his, and pleasure flashed through every nerve of my body at the sound of my name in his mouth. His expression, however, was serious. Worried, even.

"Alexandre."

"The spirit that follows you, that hurts you. It is *not* your sister."

Not ... SuChin? I began to respond, but then the door was pulled open—I hadn't even known we'd stopped—and a strange man poked his head into the coach.

"Master DuMort! Welcome! We are so excited to have you here."

Chapter Seven

Alexandre donned his DuMort mask, pretending he did not hear the snickers and snide murmurs from the aristocrats surrounding us. The house was a mansion, lit bright with chandeliers laden with Hanzo wax candles, burning with such a blue-white brilliance they couldn't be stared at directly. This light reflected from many priceless Arshbiri tapestries, woven of precious metals beat into the finest of threads, so that the marble floors scintillated like they were veined with diamonds.

All but the servants wore formal wear and masks. Bejewelled and feathered and iridescent-scaled though they were, the masks were not mere frivolity as they might be at a ball: like mine, they hid features, and in this hiding revealed dark truths.

There was danger in this crowd, a menace that prowled unseen from one pearl-embroidered skirt to another Rovana silk suit. The women's smiles were sharp as an executioner's blades, and the men ... they wore no weapons, but their hands lingered close to their pockets. Damning acts would be committed this night, and I prayed to the heavens and saints that they would only belong to DuMort.

If DuMort was aware of danger, I saw no sign. I did not yet know him well enough to understand the messages in his body: the stiffness of his nimble fingers, the slow blink of his dark lashes when he looked at me. Were it not for his warning in the carriage, I might have thought him placid as we were led to a darkened room with a single candle. The two dozen or so onlookers followed behind, blocking us from the door. Staring behind their extravagant masks. Mocking us in voices barely lowered.

He spoke to me in DongTi, and it was only because he announced each step to the onlookers, and from some familiarity, that I knew which tools to prepare. I was careful to remain at his side, feigning incomprehension, until the gibberish that was once my mother tongue was said.

The guests pushed closer as he read fortunes and conjured the dead. They were insulting in their cynicism, peeking under the table prepared for him and knocking at the rectangular trays I set out, looking for secret devices. Slowly, patient as a spider, DuMort wove his web and enraptured them all.

He channelled their dead until tears streamed down rouged cheeks, until throats roughened with suppressed emotion cleared once, twice. Noses were blown. The snide comments ceased, until only one voice spoke, unfurling across the polished marble floors to rattle upwards through skeletons and into ears. They stared at the occultist's pulsing dark presence like he might save them all.

I longed for the show to be over: I was tired from the sleepless night and long days; the skin between my shoulder blades fair crawled with dread; the mask chafed against the scratches on my face until I was sure I wept blood. Most of all, I longed to question Alexandre about my sister's shade.

Only he'd said it wasn't her.

He'd seen something behind me today. The same shadowy spirit that followed me everywhere; the same one that first appeared to me a handful of years ago, months after the DongTi traders I'd paid to find my sister reported her dead.

"She died earlier this year, Lady," one of the men had reported. "Sudden and unexpected, her neighbour said. A childbirth gone wrong."

I had stared down at the pale grey of my gown, waiting for the scarlet of my blood to stain the silk, a sign my ribcage was splitting open like a screaming mouth. Surely no mere flesh and bone could withstand the emotions exploding inside me: the grief of losing SuChin twisting with the regret of not finding her sooner; the blasphemous desire to cry out for my older sister and knowing that to do so might damn her to earthly suffering.

Beautiful and kind SuChin was gone.

My sister.

Dismay ran like molten earth through me. Why hadn't she come to find me? Perhaps, like me, she thought her only sibling dead. What cruelties would she have had to endure, what depraved conditions did she survive, an abandoned child of thirteen summers with nothing, absolutely nothing in the world except a vengeful spirit and her father's remains? I'd thought of her daily, as I washed floors and scrubbed clothing and wept from exhaustion. At least I'd had my mother, and then when she'd died suddenly one night, the lady of the house had shown me unbelievable kindness. I'd hoped the same fortune would find SuChin, and if not, I prayed death found her swiftly. It was the only mercy I could think of that remained to her.

She had survived all those years, by some miracle. The moment she was within my reach, my grim prayers had been answered and cruel gods had stolen my sister from me.

"My Lady?" one of the traders I'd hired said.

I do not know how long I sat there, staring at the front of my dress like a fool. Waiting for my flesh to sunder under the force of my grief. But no speck of blood darkened the light grey silk—only tears.

She would have been forty. The age my mother was when she was widowed, when she left all she knew to save her daughters.

"Thank you," I managed, and slipped the pouch of coins into one of the trader's hands as I fled.

SuChin's spirit had appeared in my room that very night, a blurred, silent shadow, dripping with ill intent. At first I'd borne it: after all, it was what I deserved. I should have jumped from the boat after her. I should have pled with the captain, or my mother. I should have done anything but freeze stupidly, watching her small form shrink into nothing as we left her behind.

The dim room brightened suddenly, and I blinked away my own tears. DuMort was finished, and he spoke to the guests while I hurried to gather the offerings and ready to leave.

"Where do these go, then?" A man grabbed the tray I reached for. The clump of flesh slid across the wooden surface, a gelatinous snail I did not wish to identify. "Your master's blood price."

I shook my head and shrugged, repeating the few words I still remembered my mother saying. *Come here, Mi Nga. Time to sleep. I love you, my daughter.*

Though I'd last seen DuMort across the room, surrounded by admirers, somehow he was at my side in an instant. "My assistant cannot answer questions," he told the guest politely. "Perhaps I may help?"

The man looked appraisingly at me, at my modern, Western dress and masquerade mask that matched the others. "Just making conversation," he smirked. "Making a foreigner feel welcome, like any good citizen."

DuMort bowed in gratitude, and I hurried to imitate his

gesture, releasing my skirts from the curtsy I had begun. "Mydalla has treated this occultist most kindly," DuMort said. "And now, we must hurry to our next engagement."

He took hold of my arm and led me across the dim room, towards the scintillating hallway. The onlookers parted before us, giving us easy access to the doorway. The sense of menace was still there, but there was also a deference in the house that hadn't been at our arrival. Perhaps it was for the guests' lost loved ones; perhaps it was for DuMort, who'd channelled them. DuMort's hand on me was firm, his palm moist. I understood from his grip that, somehow, the scales might tip to violence at any moment.

We had reached the front door, and Alexandre muttered so that only my ear caught his words. "You remember the way to the carriage?"

I nodded.

"If I am not in sight within five minutes of your arrival, my driver will leave. And you are not to argue, understand? I will send a carriage to fetch you tomorrow morning."

"Is it the Socie—"

The words died in my mouth at his suppressing glare. Alexandre gave me a gentle push out the mansion doors, and then he spoke with DuMort's charm again. "Now, we are rather in a rush, so let me bid a quick goodbye to our host and be on my way."

I walked down the long walkway, fighting the urge to run. Fighting the urge to turn back for Alexandre. Why couldn't he have left with me—why had he bothered staying? The night was dark and the street lanterns hissed. Damp fog soaked my black slippers and chilled the sheen of sweat on my skin. All was quiet at this late hour, with few carriages and fewer pedestrians. This was a safe area, regularly patrolled by guards, but I hadn't felt so vulnerable in years. I saw Alexandre's carriage waiting where we'd left it, three streets away, and his driver climbed down to let me in. He looked past me, down the street, and then spoke tersely. "We leave in five minutes. Am I taking you to your home?"

I nodded. "Unless Alexandre joins us."

He nodded and closed the carriage door, his eyes still staring down the street as he did. Fatigue and fear filled my bones, and even the warm blanket in the coach did little to temper my shaking. I had left another person behind to save myself. I was a coward, an utterly useless coward.

What could I have done to help, a part of me wondered. He was a grown man, and he'd told me to go—had pushed me through the door himself. And yet ... perhaps the Braithewaite name would have seen us come to no harm. Perhaps a woman might have wrung mercy from the Society Men.

The carriage jolted as its wheels began to turn. Had five minutes passed so quickly? I looked out the window, but there was no hunched man running beside us. The decision had been taken from me.

Alexandre was experienced and capable. And Mydallan nobles were civilised, more apt to stab one in the back with poisoned words than with a knife. He would be held longer than he wished, answering questions and entertaining, and then he'd be released unharmed.

Or given to the gendarmes.

My heart stopped at the thought, my blood congealing within my veins. They couldn't call the gendarmes—the hosts and all guests would be considered accomplices. I had to believe that, or I'd be imagining the occultist hanging from a noose, his glorious, liquid gown moving despite his lifeless body.

The intricately carved alabaster columns lining my husband's property appeared, as joyless as prison bars. I took the tools and offerings of my occultist with me and nodded solemnly to his driver as I walked the long path to my home.

The night passed, agonisingly slow. I slept in fits and spurts, seeing sharp teeth and masks weeping blood. I dreamt of SuChin as she was, as I remembered her, but her ghost did not visit me. I almost wished for her: Edgar's genteel snores and the loud ticking of the grandfather clock in the hallway did little for my solitude.

In the morning, I sipped cup after cup of tea on the balcony as the sun rose over Mydalla. Edgar hid behind his newsprint wall, and I read the front page headlines. There was no mention of an arrested occultist. He hadn't been turned to the gendarmes then.

"Will you stop that, please?" Edgar said.

"Hmm?"

"That is a handmade porcelain teacup, and you're rattling it onto its saucer like a spinster having a spell."

I set my tea onto the table and pressed my shaking hands into my lap. Eventually, when the red-tinted sun was high, Edgar folded up his newspaper and went inside, and the servants cleared up our breakfast and called me down for lunch. I ignored them, staring down at the street, afraid to visit the toilet in case I missed Alexandre's carriage.

The sun set. I ignored calls for dinner, shivering in the cool dusk with only my regrets to keep me warm.

His carriage never came.

Alexandre had disappeared.

Chapter Eight

Two a.m. found me knocking at the entrance of Alexandre's apartment, holding a sac of food taken from my own pantries. Waves from the nearby harbour crashed dark brine upon salt-rimed docks, heaved boat against boat, water droplets leaping into the air from each impact. The buildings closest to the churning sea were speckled with ice, jutting from their weathered walls like broken teeth. Guilt drove the blade of my fist hard against the door. No movement sounded from within. The wind slid beneath my heavy cloak, grazing cold fingers through my skirts and between my buttons. I shivered and hammered again.

The landlady came, cursing and yawning. She scowled at me, so fiercely it took my breath away. Rarely have I seen such a baleful look cast so openly in my direction.

"He's not here." Her voice was raspy with sleep, filled with venom.

"I know." I pointed at the stairs. "I don't know when he will return, but his wife is ill, and I wanted to make sure someone has checked on her." While I mooned about in the comfort of my home, refusing meals like a fretful titmouse,

Alexandre's wife had been left unfed and uncared for. What would he think of me once he found out?

She grimaced. "His wife? Why's he bringing the likes of *you* home then?"

I drew myself up to my full height: even so, I reached only her chin. "Has someone come by or not, madam? If not, I suggest you allow me in, or deal with a possible death in your rooms."

There was a roar from down the street, a loud splash. The woman opened the door wider. "That's old Taggart, in his cups again." She cursed and pulled her threadbare robe tighter around her neck, sliding past me onto the street. "He'll drown himself in the horse trough if someone doesn't pull him out."

The landlady looked back over her shoulder as she hurried into the night's cold embrace. "Go on up then, and check on your lover's wife." There was a sneer in her voice, a contempt that heated my cheeks and raised my ire, but I said nothing.

My feet knew their way up these narrow, creaky steps, even in the dark. I opened the door to his apartment, bringing with me the lantern that hung outside. "Madam DuMort?" I ventured.

There was no reply. Without Alexandre's presence here, the place felt empty. He'd left the far window open, and early winter's chill had crept in. The tea we'd left unfinished in our cups held a patina of ice: I moved these to the small sink and placed my sack of food onto the table before turning towards the rooms.

My breath clouded as it left my body, white and fleeting as a ghost, and I shivered again. Alexandre's wife must be freezing. I realised I didn't even know her first name.

The last door on the right, the one he usually closed when I came calling, lay ajar. No light flickered from the room, nor any sound came to my ears. I walked there with a slow, exaggerated stride, nearly marching, so that my footsteps announced my approach. I did not wish to alarm her.

"Madam DuMort, I'm Alexandre's assistant. Do you need anything? I've brought some food."

I shut the window against the cold and turned to the door. My hands trembled as I reached for the handle, lantern held high. I would finally meet the woman who held Alexandre's heart. The woman who, if not for her, might allow us to be togeth—

The bed was empty.

Nothing stirred as I entered. Not a voice answered mine, nor was there an answering cloud of breath from another's lungs. The plain bed was made: not neatly, not as a maid would, but uncaringly, as a matter of habit. I paced the small area carefully, lantern sweeping left to right, worried she had fallen between what must be their wheeled traveling trunk and the apartment's armoire.

There was no one in the room, nor in the bathroom across the hall. Had the Society Men, not content with capturing Alexandre, come to take his wife as well? Yet there was no sign of a struggle: surely they would not have made the bed she'd lain in prior to stealing her away like a changeling. I paced the room again, thoughts swirling like the sea outside.

My lantern paused at the armoire, and a strange compulsion slithered through my body. I opened the doors, the hinges groaning like tortured mice, and looked inside. Alexandre's strange clothing hung, the black shirts and long gowns that absorbed the shadows, ever-shifting beneath my flickering flame. I brushed my fingertips across them, pressed my nose close to inhale Alexandre's familiar, smoky scent, wishing I could be so bold when their owner wore them. I sent a fervent prayer to the gods and saints above that the occultist was safe.

Something rounded and beige, slightly larger than a curled-up child, hid in the bottom of the armoire. I knelt upon the cold floor, placing the lantern nearby so I might see, and reached for it slowly.

It was merely a large laundry sack, stuffed with clothing, and relief loosened my bones. No doubt he was due for a trip to a laundress. I pulled out Alexandre's voluminous, dark outfits, and flushed hot at his white underthings. There was a dark imprint on one of his shirts that looked like a woman's open mouth—his wife's lip lacquer, perhaps? I brought it to my own face, closer to the flame, to examine this first hint of his wife's appearance, but I was mistaken. The stain was no ordinary pigment a woman might wear: it smelled of sickly sweetness and rusted copper.

It smelled of blood.

I shoved it back into the bag, my skin crawling. No doubt the occultist had spilled a vial while performing his mysterious rituals over the flesh payments. The metallic odour had awakened my senses dulled from the late hour, or I'd tilted my head just right, for I became aware of a foul smell emanating from the other corner of the closet.

The lantern flame illuminated a newspaper-wrapped package, about the size of my fist. Even in the dim light I could see it oozed. A sour, bitter taste seeped into my mouth and my stomach heaved at the stench—wet decay and liquid horrors, overlaid by a heavy saccharine perfume that compounded my revulsion.

I dared not touch it; I dared not ignore it. My unsatiated curiosity would burrow into the growing fruit of our friendship like a worm, weakening it from the very core. I grimaced at the thought of what I might find beneath the sodden paper and ink, imagined being reminded of it every morning as Edgar took his breakfast on the balcony, safe behind his newsprint wall. Was a question with no answer better than a cruel lesson? To that end: was an infatuation that remained unconsummated better than a guilty conscience?

The front door opened, and I leapt to my feet, closing the armoire doors and straightening my skirts. "Is someone there?" I called out, as though I owned the place.

There was no answer.

I took the lantern and stepped into the hallway, expecting to see the sullen landlady or Madam DuMort. The firelight danced shadows upon the walls but did not reach the door.

"Hello?" My voice faltered and my steps grew heavier as I neared the foyer.

The edge of my light reached a figure, standing just to the side of the door. I dared not breathe as the lantern revealed dark shoes; a long, lean form. A face so wreathed in darkness, it looked like a skull.

"Alexandre," I cried, and rushed towards him. Intending what, I do not know—a hand clasp, a touch of his cheek, an embrace—but all was denied me by the stark fear on his face, more immobilising than the icy wind of a winter night. And then the expression was gone, wiped away with the last layer of shadow, and only exhaustion hung on his gaunt features.

"Mina. What are you doing here?" His voice was strained, but there was no anger in it.

"You disappeared. I didn't know when you'd return. I thought to check on your wife." My words tumbled over each other, so many thoughts and feelings fighting to be expressed at once. His eyes flicked to the open door of their bedroom. "But she was not here."

He nodded, brow furrowed, and sat heavily upon a chair.

"Your landlady did not know of her existence," I pressed further. At first I thought I did so for words of praise, like a pathetic mongrel, but my need was higher, more dignified that that: I wanted answers.

Alexandre nodded again, and his face grew still more troubled. I fought the urge to comfort him, to smooth the deep lines from his skin, but softness would get me nowhere.

"There are only men's clothes in the armoire." The matter of the paper-bound package in the armoire floated up between us. I treated it as I would any other foul stench in polite company: I ignored it, more concerned with other matters. "There was blood on one of your undershirts."

He did not move at all. He might have been a statue, a hare frozen upon a predator's approach, but for the incessant silken rasp of his ever-moving gown.

I gripped hard the lantern in my hand, its handle slippery in my damp palm. "Alexandre. Where. Is. Your. Wife?"

He shook his head. "We must leave Mydalla, Mina. We do not have much time."

The thought of life without him silenced my next questions, chased them down my throat, past liver and spleen and stomach until I lost them entirely.

"You're leaving?" I repeated. "So soon?" Nothing had changed during Alexandre's time here: not that which haunted me, nor my empty marriage, yet I could not imagine returning to the life I'd lived just a fortnight ago. It was as if I'd tasted the most succulent dishes, richly spiced and perfectly prepared. His abandonment sentenced me to a diet of stale bread once more.

Even the most tame of women would not accept such a fate willingly.

<h1 style="text-align:center">Chapter Nine</h1>

He passed a weary hand over his eyes and muttered, as if to himself. "Our time together is running out, and I have yet to achieve what I desire."

My legs grew weak with his admission. He was strained beyond exhaustion, and in such cases, private thoughts were apt to slip out. Was he finally putting into words all that lay between us?

"Tell me of your desire," I said, as softly as an exhaled breath against one's ear, as gentle as a trembling touch against one's bare skin.

"It involves you, of course." His dark eyes fixed on his wife's doorway, and he grimaced as if the admission pained him. "I have done evil things, Mina. Broken the laws of man and nature. I have committed sins that a demon would be loathe to admit."

"There must have been good reason behind them." I pressed myself against the rickety side table. If I took one wrong step, this tenuous spell between us might be broken.

"There is nothing that can justify ... at the time, in the heat of the moment ... my intentions were good." He snapped his gaze onto mine. "Whatever happens, whatever you learn. Please. It's important you know that."

"I do." I nodded fervently. "I trust you."

Alexandre laughed mirthlessly. "You shouldn't. You know nothing about me. The rituals I've performed, blasphemies against gods and men. I am damned."

His face grew sombre. "I am doomed."

"Is it the Society Men? What did they do to you last night?"

His elegant hand swatted away my questions. "Forget about them. Our time together is short,"—oh, the pang in my heart at those words!—"and I promised to help you with your ghost." He cast his eyes around me, frowning in concentration. "But where is it? I saw something yesterday." He cursed. "I am drained. I've not slept all night. I need rest, and sustenance."

"Of course," I murmured. "I have left your tools at my house, at any rate."

"All?" He frowned.

"Everything." His silence pressed against me, pushing explanations from my mouth. "I was thinking of you all day, you see, and then I thought of your poor wife, and came over here immediately, bringing only food." I gestured to the sack on the table.

"You are so kind, Mina." His velvet voice was gruff. "A better friend to us than many have been to you, no doubt."

He had seen to the very heart of me, had named the unspoken yearning I carried on my shoulders like the heaviest of burdens: since my mother had died, and save for Edgar's distracted affections, I had not a friend in the world. It was ridiculous, truly. My life was more than a servant's orphaned child could ever dream of, and yet I complained that I was *lonely*.

The unexpected clarity with which he saw me pierced

through my fragile shell, destroying the crumbling facade that weakened with every dream I kept to myself, every fear left unnamed, every moment I felt uncared for. My face burned, the scratches on my face throbbing anew. They seemed to gape open like repulsive mouths, my features foreign and grotesque under Alexandre's steady gaze.

I dared not meet his eyes, staring instead at the scarred wooden floor between us. "There is something ... wrong ... with me. It drives people away." Beneath my dress, my stomach dropped at my admission, but I knew it to be true. Edgar did not permit me to befriend the servants, but surely amongst the Mydallan upper class there were women who might have accepted me, were it not for some intolerable flaw I could not see.

His voice was gentle, though they did not say the reassuring words my ears yearned to hear. "I made a promise to help you, and I intend to keep it. But I will need my tools."

I nodded and spoke no further: I'd said far too much on this cursed night. Something about the occultist drew my trust like a spindle pulling thread, despite the strange things about him. He would soon be gone. I only needed him to rid me of my ghost, and nothing more.

Nothing more, I told my aching heart.

Alexandre fetched his driver, and as we rode through the quiet streets, the sky lightening to grey, he lifted his chin at the horizon. "What is that short black tower, beside the four grey ones?"

I didn't bother to look as I spoke. After all, the Bastille was made to avert the eye, a dreadful narrow tower made of black steel, pocked with holes where the metal had decayed. It wept with rust, and squatted like a necrotic stump beside the four elegant crematorium spires. Even those who lived in the grimmest parts of Mydalla turned away from the sight of the "Dead Thumb", as the street urchins called it.

"This is the gendarmes' prison, for those who dare break the city's most sacred law," I said. I swallowed with difficulty: that was to be my fate, if I was ever caught with an occultist, much less assisting in his performance. Perhaps it was not too late to leave things, instead of gambling on luck and strangers' silence for any longer.

Alexandre nodded. "It looks quite different from the other buildings. I suppose that's by design."

I looked closely at him then, unsure if he had purposely made a joke. He gave me a small, nearly imperceptible wink, and my heart fluttered. The fear the Bastille imposed upon my person left me, and as I relaxed back against the coach seat, Alexandre told me of the Society Men.

"They're in every city, really: guilds of charlatans and believers both, fleecing the populace. They don't welcome traveling occultists, especially those with renown, and seek to discredit them. It's bad for business, you see, and especially in Mydalla, where they are at special risk."

I nodded. Before I'd heard of DuMort, I'd hired—and fired—many of them. "They took you?"

He leaned back against the coach bench, air escaping his voluminous clothing with a hiss. "Nothing so far as that, though the threat of force implied. They insisted I go with them to a secret meeting of 'occult professionals', despite the later performance I told them I must attend."

"Where did they take you?" I imagined a filthy, rat-infested alleyway, reeking like the soaked parcel in Alexandre's armoire. There was no point in asking him: in the same way he had deflected all questions of his sick wife, I knew he would not tell me the truth.

"A lecture hall," he chuckled, as the wan light from the rising sun illuminated his sallow skin and fatigue-bruised eyes. "They sat me at a table in the centre, bright candles surrounding me while they remained seated in the shadows. They tested me for hours."

"Tested?" I was bewildered. "What kind of tests?"

"Questions about their dead." He rubbed a hand from his sternum to navel, as if comforting himself. "Endlessly. They were drunk, or otherwise inebriated, and wanted me to fail. Then they'd be in their rights to rid their town of a fraud, I imagine."

"But you did not fail." I was certain he wouldn't. From all I had seen, all he had shown me: Alexandre was no fraud.

"I did not, though my conduit and I are near death with exhaustion."

The carriage drew to a stop at the Braithwaite gates. Distantly, I saw Edgar on our balcony, and for once the newspaper did not obscure his face. "Your conduit is near death? I thought it was already of the spirit world."

Alexandre gave me a wan smile. "Permit this old fraud his exaggerations."

"You are neither a fraud, nor old," I protested, but I was not certain. Though his face might belong to a man anywhere in his twenties, or fifties, and he had thick, dark hair untouched by grey, Alexandre possessed a quality I'd only seen in the elderly. A frailty to his posture, a gingerness to his movements, as if he was burdened with a constant pain.

"I've lived a thousand lives, died a thousand deaths, and still the people clamour for more." He settled himself more comfortably on the stage bench, pulling the fur blanket more securely on his lap. "I will await my tools, and the flesh payments."

"Are we going somewhere else?" I glanced over my shoulder. Edgar stood at the balcony railing, stance wide. His anger traversed the distance between us: over the dew-drenched grass of our gardens through the fading remnants of the night's mist, tightening my shoulders as if gripped by disapproving hands.

"You may sleep in your own home, or you may rest in our apartment. Whatever you wish," Alexandre said. "But I need my things."

I nodded. "I will bring them right away."

The walk towards my front door was an eternity. My husband's ire grew more intense as I neared: I winced as I approached the inferno, but my steps did not slow.

A maid opened the door and stared at her feet as I passed. The house was silent as a mausoleum, the servants scurrying from my approach like frightened mice.

Respect, if not love, drove me to see Edgar first. I walked through our bedroom and onto the chill balcony. There was only one cup on the tray, one plate, one napkin. Edgar paced the length of the narrow space, pale face mottled.

For a long moment, neither of us spoke.

And then he did, and I wished immediately he hadn't. "How dare you show your face here as if you've done nothing wrong." My husband bit off each word, sharp and jagged. They pierced my skin as they reached me.

"It's my home too." There was no point in denial: though my body had not known another man's touch, I would not have spurned Alexandre's advances. In fact, I yearned for them.

"And it's *my* good name you've been dragging through the mud. It would be one thing if you'd wanted a discreet affair— gods know I wouldn't have cared—but to traipse about town all night with a criminal?"

"You wouldn't have cared if I loved another?" I knew this, had told myself so many times, and yet I found myself blinking back tears. Once I was his, and he mine, and there was no one who could turn our gaze from each other. Now, his gaze was fixed away from me, blind and uncaring.

His answer reached my ears, barely audible through the rushing of blood in my head. "I have no control over your heart, but I deserve your respect. After everything I've risked and put up with to marry you—the very least you could have done was protect the name that protected you all these years."

"You married me because you said you loved me."

"I did love you. Despite the fact you were DongTi."

"Despite ...?"

I took a step away from the man who was once my husband, away from the expression on his face. He was repulsed by me, by my actions, and wanted me to know it.

Edgar's words severed what remained of our marriage, cast me adrift from the only person who might care if I lived or died.

Without him, I was utterly unloved in this world.

A strange frenzy overtook my limbs at this truth, a silent shriek that I contained within my lockbox of flesh and bone, and I hurried away from the balcony on which we'd watched so many sunrises, from the bed where we'd made promises and confessions in equal measure, from the man who swore he'd love me forever.

With shaking legs I stumbled to a nearby guest bedroom, and from the back of an empty drawer, I pulled out the bag that contained Alexandre's occult paraphernalia. I had found a man to care for me once: I would do so again, and his love would fill this aching void that sucked the very air from my lungs.

Edgar called to me as I fled down the stairs. "Where do you think you're going?"

I did not answer. I couldn't. If I opened my mouth, the shriek inside me would rip me apart, tear flesh from sinew and marrow from bone, rendering me a weeping heap on our pristine marble floors. Instead, I bit my lips closed with my front teeth, and set my eyes where Alexandre's carriage awaited me in the distance.

As Edgar bellowed at me, a maid moved towards the front door, her eyes averted from my face. I had a moment of worry, but rather than bar my escape, she opened the door with a small curtsy.

I could not thank her.

Chapter Ten

Sorrow nestled, thick as blood, in my throat, but I could not weep. Alexandre watched as his driver helped me into the carriage; he asked no questions, merely furrowed his fine brow at the expression on my face, and unburdened from me his bag of supplies.

The ride back was slower, the roads busier. Men drove stinking wagons of night soil towards the city gates, women gave hoarse-voiced cries from the sides of the road to sell their wares, and bored-looking merchants rode rickshaws or coaches towards the city centre. Disbelief darkened my sight like a passing cloud. How could these people continue about their day? The world as I knew it was destroyed: my marriage ended, Alexandre prepared to depart, and I was once again cast adrift in dangerous waters, forced to leave my home.

I stiffened as the idea came to me. It was beneath me, of course, but desperation drove even the most righteous of us to our knees. Alexandre had performed cursed rituals, he'd said. And no doubt SuChin had been forced to perform acts that did not sit well in her soul, just to survive. Perhaps that was why her spirit could not ascend with the others, why it was so angry with ... But it was not SuChin that haunted me, Alexandre had said.

I'd been saved from performing unsavoury acts my whole life: first by my mother, who roughened her hands and knees scrubbing floors to feed us, and then by the Lady Summerhill, who took me in when Mother died. And then Edgar ... but I turned my thoughts from him. I needed another saviour.

Alexandre would not be moved to take me with him when he left Mydalla, not when he already had an assistant awaiting his return. A person of his character would require another, stronger reason to bring me. A man burdened with a sick wife may well be as unfulfilled as a woman burdened with a distant husband. If I could only make him see that what he felt for me was reciprocated, that I would welcome his embrace with discreetly open arms ...

"Mina," he said, and I looked at him guiltily. Had his conduit told him what was in my mind?

He gestured to the carriage door. With a start I saw it was open, the traffic that had surrounded us replaced by familiar port buildings, hoarse merchants' cries replaced by shrill gulls, and his driver waiting to help me down.

His landlady sneered when she saw me, and I flinched, wishing fervently that she'd return to pretending I did not exist. "Didn't find his wife, I guess?"

"Madame Ro, please," Alexandre chided her, and she subsided. Her eyes bore holes between my shoulder blades as I ascended up the narrow staircase.

And then we were alone in his apartment. For the first time, I understood that there was no one behind the bedroom door to witness what might follow.

I turned to him as he shut the door carefully, but he moved around me, his wild gown sliding against the wall with a whispering hush, the glass bottles in his sack of flesh payments clinking like fine glass flutes at a wedding. "I will be but a moment, Mina."

He disappeared into the room that belonged to his wife and closed the door. I took the time to pinch my lips into swollen rosiness, to release my long dark tresses from their careful pins. My hands wrung together, fingers of one hand soothing the other, and I waited with dry mouth and quivering stomach for the occultist to return.

He came out some minutes later, looking as he always did: features sharp as a sickle blade, eyes dark as deep shadow. As before, as always, breath fled from my lungs when I saw his face. This time, I did not hide my admiration. No, I feasted like a starving beast upon the masculine curve of his jaw, the elegant precipice of his cheekbone.

There was so little time to convince him. I moved swiftly, confidently, towards him. Wrapping my arms around his neck and raising on my toes, I finally allowed myself to press my lips against his.

I expected a moment of hesitation, had girded myself to withstand the frozen shock he might display before he melted into my embrace.

I was unprepared for the strength of his reaction.

He shoved me away without hesitation, almost brutally. I lost my balance and fell to the ground at his feet.

My knees felt bruised, but that was nothing compared to my pride, and I stared downwards, seeing nothing, while heat scorched every inch of my skin. It was not passion that enflamed me, but humiliation; not shyness that kept my eyes downcast, but shame.

He knelt to the ground an arm's length from me, but did not move closer. The silver chain he always wore escaped from his gown and hung suspended in the air. A locket dangled from it.

Alexandre's words were hard, but his voice was tender.

"You're better than that. You're a married woman, and I'm a married man."

I swallowed hard, the taste in my mouth turned bitter, but I had come this far. "Because of my association with you, I am no longer married. And as for you—where is your wife?"

He gestured towards his chest. "She is always with me. Here."

At his second refusal of me, my tears fell in earnest, splattering upon his rented wooden floors. What of the connection I'd felt between us, the bond that had made me feel loved and whole? How could I have imagined it all?

Alexandre pressed his white handkerchief into my hand, murmuring comforts in my mother tongue. Perhaps it was his proximity to my people that drew me towards him: but no, even the graceful creases that made up his knuckles; the curve of his fingernails, rusty with old blood; the blue-grey veins like lines of sapphire buried beneath his skin; all were beautiful to me.

I took a deep, shuddering breath and stood up, staring down at my boots.

He stood also, and with gentle fingers lifted my chin to meet his gaze once more. There was no sign of judgment in his eyes, no smirk or sneer that would have shattered me. There was only kindness, understanding, and that look which I had mistaken for affection.

"There is something you must know," he said.

A yell from below and the heavy tromp of many boots thundered up the stairs like a frantic drumbeat.

Alexandre swooped towards his door, but in vain: it was thrown open, cracking as it hit the wall, and the uniforms of the gendarmes flooded the apartment, a tidal wave of dark blue cloth and deep voices.

They grabbed him, and me, and were none too gentle as they did. They dragged me out first, past the snarl of men gripping the occultist, and Alexandre surged in my direction, slipping something cold and heavy into my bodice with his quick hands. A foul smell accompanied his movement, foul and sickly sweet, and I could not help but recoil.

The object slid to a stop between my bound breasts, and I prayed there was no outwards sign of it that the gendarmes might see.

My boots brushed the steps but did not touch ground once as they hauled me out the doors. The glint of the silver carriages sparked a fear in me that I'd learned from childhood: *silver coaches for those who will never be saved/ the police fill prison cells while the gendarmes dig graves.*

There was no crowd to watch my arrest: the gendarmes were too feared, their prisoners too pitied, for such behavior. And so it was that my eye could not help but fall upon the lone figure standing on the deserted cobblestone street. A figure that had no business being in this part of town, let alone present for this horrible turn of events. One of the men holding me doffed his hat at the man.

And my once-husband, Lord Edgar Braithwaite, nodded back.

Chapter Eleven

The silver carriage rattled along my bones and up my spine, vibrating my organs into a churning mess. At the start of the ride, I'd met the eye of the uniformed man opposite me, hoping to see pity or curiosity. There was nought but contempt on his face. I kept my gaze upon my bound hands, gripping each other like scared children on my lap, from then on. The men's stinking breath, loud voices, and over-close bodies made me shrink more tightly into myself.

When the vehicle stopped and the door opened, I was dragged roughly into the cold, bright daylight. I did not look up.

There was no need to. The wind shrieking through the holes in the black steel like the screams of tormented souls told me where they'd brought me.

I was at the Bastille.

The heavy metal door squealed on anguished hinges as the gendarmes shoved me into the dark entrance, the shrill chorus almost drowning out the clatter of metal carriage wheels. I twisted to look behind me, at Alexandre, but it was only the coach that had brought me speeding away, as if the gendarmes themselves could not bear being so near the Dead Thumb. DuMort's silver carriage had not arrived.

Strong hands took hold of my upper arms and pulled me forwards, but all was darkness. "One moment," I pleaded. "I can't see." My jailers paused, allowing me to blink until my eyes grew accustomed to the dim light.

"I'm ready, thank you." My calm words were betrayed by the tremble in my voice.

They dragged me towards an open doorway of opaque black; crossing this threshold felt like entering the underworld itself, where our priests said the unAscended souls that dared speak of the dead remained trapped in their rotting corpses, feeling their own bodies decay in pure, unending agony. The air was stale and chill, moist and cloying against my exposed skin. I retched at the odour: human waste and unwashed bodies and an even worse smell I could not put name to.

There were many stairs, so many I lost count, so many I gulped at the foul air as if it were the finest of wines. There was no light, save where weather had left pockmarks in the dark metal, and what those rare beams illuminated—the hopeless despair on the faces we passed—made me weep. Silently at first, a tear trickled down my cheek in pity. And as we passed more and more cells, as I understood that this was to be *my* fate: that I was no longer Lady Mina Braithewaite, but another forgotten wretch; that my own face would be staring uncaringly at the next prisoner the gendarmes brought in; wracking sobs overtook my body. The strong hands that gripped either side of me were all that kept me upright. Their footsteps were steady and unhesitating: my jailers were able to see in this blackness, like the rats I heard skittering away at our approach.

"I don't belong here!" I cried out, and my voice echoed back to my ears, distorted and mocking. "Please, release me."

One of my jailers leaned close to my ear. "Certainly." A woman's voice, cold and hard as the steel surrounding us.

Sudden, wild hope ceased my tears. "You'll ... let me go?"

"Of course." The woman yanked me up another dozen steps. "Your cell is right here."

They shoved me into a tiny space no larger than my closet. My arms, numbed by the strength of their grip, tingled with pain when they finally unhanded me. It was utterly dark, save for the thinnest sunbeam shining through a hole in the cell beside mine. With this most meagre of light, I could make out a thin pad on the rough stone floor that was to serve as my bed, and a chamberpot in the corner that churned my stomach with its reek.

"Change." The woman's voice spoke. "Your uniform is on your cot."

I mustered up my haughtiest voice. "I am fine in my dress, thank you."

"Change." The man's voice this time, coming from the taller silhouette. "Or we'll change you."

There was no partition in the tiny cell, not even a screen behind which I might find privacy. The darkness was my only cover, and I turned my back to my jailers and changed quickly. Something clinked onto the floor as I removed dress, and too late I remembered Alexandre's lunge towards me and the coolness of metal he'd slipped between my breasts.

One of the guards' shadows bent to pick it up off the ground. "You'll get your locket and other personal effects back the day of your release."

Alexandre had given me his locket. What message might he have slipped inside? Despair pricked my eyes with tears and made my breath ragged.

"Please, I'd like to wear the necklace. It holds great, personal meaning for me," I said, hopelessly.

"Don the uniform," the man's voice instructed, as if I hadn't spoken.

I pulled the rough material over my head: it rubbed

painfully against the healing scratches on my face and itched where it rested on my body. It was thin, but mercifully odourless: without my layers of skirts and undergarments, the Bastille's chill raised gooseflesh on my skin.

They left when I handed my dress through a space in the bars, their synchronous footsteps and mocking banter floating back to my ears as they descended down the spiral tower stairs.

My legs shook as I stood in the dark, shook until my fists gripping the cell bars vibrated, shook until I sank to my knees on the cold floor. This couldn't be happening. My husband could not have betrayed me so, even if he believed I betrayed him. I needed Alexandre. He would know what to do, or at the very least was a sympathetic ear.

I strained my ears impatiently for the twin footsteps that would signal the jailers bringing in another prisoner, but all I heard were wet coughs and mutters from the prisoners below me. The force of my fierce yearning should have summoned the occultist to me: I pictured his face in my mind and *willed* it to appear, pictured it rising out of the darkness like a swimmer floating to the surface of a lake. My own face heated as I remembered our last moment together: how I'd made a fool of myself and he'd pushed me so firmly away. That humiliation was nothing compared to this new reality.

I'd relive that moment a thousand times if it would release me from the Dead Thumb.

Though it was surely no later than early afternoon, I could not remain in this moment. Unable to trust my legs, I crawled to the thin mat that was to be my bed. It reeked of mildew and old urine. I curled upon it anyway, pulling the coarse blanket over me and closing my eyes, swollen from weeping.

I sought the only escape that remained to me. I fell asleep.

～

Something crawled into my slack mouth, waking me. I tried to close my jaws, to spit whatever it was out, to no avail. My mouth was forced wide open, jaws cracking painfully, as something pushed its way down my throat. I couldn't breathe. My eyes flew open but the utter darkness kept me blind. I gave a muffled scream, and grabbed at whatever invaded my mouth.

My panicked, slapping hands met a pocket of icy air, and I understood.

The spirit I thought was my sister had found me. Found me, and meant to climb inside my body. I had no air to speak, my strength waning, but I *willed* the XieLin to depart.

As before, thank the saints, my attention was enough of a ward. The presence in my mouth faded, none too soon, and I lurched up, gasping for breath and vomiting onto the floor. A patch of blackness darker than the shadows floated away from me to squat in a corner of my cell.

The light shining through the hole in the tower was still bright. The sun had not yet subsided. In this grim place of forever night, my ghost need not wait for guttering candles or yawning servants to retire.

"Help!" I called out, my voice ragged and hoarse. "I need help, please!"

Footsteps trudged up the stairs, pausing some distance below me. "What do you want?"

"I ... I've had an accident. I just need a cloth to clean up, please." I waited, heart racing, eyes fixed on the corner I'd last seen the entity. Worry that I might be denied such a small request chilled me.

"You'll get it when we come 'round with your suppers." The footsteps receded once more.

I waited, afraid to move lest the ghost crept behind me in the dark. The vomit on the floor permeated the air and turned my stomach further. No one in the nearby cells complained.

After some time—minutes or hours—had passed, footsteps sounded again, along with the knocking of wood and the trickle of liquid pouring. Two jailers came up the stairs, this time carrying a thieves' lantern. The dim illumination was near blinding after so long in the dark, but it was enough to scare my violent ghost away.

The guards wore matching dark robes, their hair shorn save for a halo circling their skulls. They were priests then, or would be one day. One of them held a stack of wooden bowls and the other poured a ladle of something steaming into one. They added a slice of bread and slid it into my cell from a gap in the bars.

"Please, I need a cloth." I gestured to the puddle of sick beside my mat.

The bowl carrier tossed one towards me. It was already cold and wet, with the acrid scent of vinegar searing my nostrils. Hurriedly, while I had some light, I wiped up the mess as best I could.

"Leave it until we come to empty your chamberpot," one of the guards said.

I nodded and picked up my bowl of food, eager to please. "Thank you. When the gendarmes took me, there were two of us. Do you know what happened to my friend?"

The other snickered. "The occultist? He's too evil even for the Bastille."

"But this is where the damned are punished," I protested. "There is no place worse."

They had already moved past me, to those in the higher floors, but the guard's amused words lingered like the stench of vinegar: "There's the gallows."

Chapter Twelve

The darkness around me contained no terror worse than what roiled beneath my skin. I forced myself to eat each tasteless spoonful of my supper as if it were medicine; with every bite I forced down my ravaged throat, I swallowed a fact my mind must accept.

Edgar, my husband, had betrayed me to the gendarmes.

This was to be my new home, for however long the magistrates decided. I'd never known anyone who was sentenced to the Dead Thumb, but knew it must happen: the gendarmes' silver carriages rattled into the steel tower's yard too frequently. No one ever spoke about what happened afterwards.

I might spend my life here, or I might be exiled from the city upon my release, but the fortune Lady Summerhill had bestowed to me upon her death, the wealth I had brought into my marriage, was gone. The unAscended had no rights before the magistrates.

My spoon scraped against the near empty bowl and trembled against my front teeth. Alexandre would be executed, if he wasn't already dead. The only man who could have saved me would soon stop existing—because of *me*.

Guilt pressed against my chest, making it difficult to breathe. I slid the bowl back towards the bars and curled like a small child on the mat. Quietly, so no one could hear, I wept. At first I cried for Alexandre, who had risked everything to enter this cursed city—for what? I cursed my foolishness at losing his locket, tortured myself with what message it might have contained that might have saved us both.

Selfish regrets rose to the surface.

I mourned the life that was taken from me, the blessed life I had squandered with my desperation, the pleasures of the city I would never experience again.

As the night passed, tear by dripping tear, my thoughts turned to old wounds that never healed. I grieved for my family: All that my mother had sacrificed, including her eldest child, only for me to wind up here. She had chosen to save the wrong daughter: I was as unworthy now as back then. I had been given everything and deserved nothing, nothing but this grim fate.

Perhaps I wanted the XieLin to return, to end my misery. Let the entity take my body so that I became a ghost, ignored and hated by all. As solitary in death as I was now.

I blinked.

I had never been more alone in my life. My family was long dead, I had not a friend in the world, and my husband despised me. I had lost my wealth, my new love, and my freedom.

My worst fear, that which I had done everything to avoid, had come to pass ... and yet my heart still traitorously beat, my breath did not cease, my blood still flowed.

Still, I remained.

The guards did not visit the cells after supper: they cared not what our lowly lot did. Or perhaps, they knew that the others were too hopeless to cause any trouble. The prisoners around me did not weep or speak or even snore; their bodies were skeletal prisons that contained their cursed souls.

Dawn's first pink light shone through the hole in the tower wall and found me sitting upright. I would get answers, I promised myself. I would learn my own fate and that of Alexandre's. I would paint Edgar as a jealous husband who framed DuMort out of spite. And if the Bastille was to be my final home and resting place, then I would request books, or embroidery, or anything else that might pass the time. My mother taught me resilience, and her sacrifice would not be wasted.

When footsteps approached, I stood up and straightened the wrinkled sack that served as a uniform. "Good morning," I said politely to their stern faces.

They did not answer. As before, one ladled food into a bowl the other carried.

"I hope you had a restful night," I tried again.

Nothing.

"I would like to speak to the head guard today, if you please. I have some important questions." My cheerful facade cracked under their cold glares.

So it went with the guard who came after, emptying chamber pots and reclaiming the soiled rag from my floor. Not a flicker of compassion or a murmur of understanding escaped them.

I ate the gruel, fighting the urge to retch. My throat was still raw from yesterday's attack, and the lumpy, half-congealed texture made me gag. I gazed at my dim cell as I fought to finish the tasteless slop, and my determination waned. It hadn't yet been twenty-four hours since the gendarmes had burst into DuMort's apartments. What might twenty-four months do?

My eyes looked towards where wall met floor, where the

next cell was placed. I well knew what would become of me, given enough time.

The Bastille was cruelly designed. If the cells had been on the same level, prisoners might whisper to each other and gain solace. My neighbours were separated from me by stone walls and many steps.

I closed my eyes and thought of Alexandre to pass the long minutes. The night we first met, and all the moments since. It was painful, knowing that all the feelings that grew between us had only been nourished by me, but it was better than thinking of Edgar.

When footsteps approached again, I obediently took my empty bowl and placed it within their easy reach. How quickly we were trained, like animals.

The guards that came to my cell carried a dim lantern, but no food. My throat tightened as they slid the key into the lock, and I retreated until my shoulder blades hit stone.

"What's going on?" I asked.

One of them stepped inside, hulking in the tiny space. She thrust a bundle into my sweating palm. "Change," she said.

I frowned and shook out the bundle. It was the dress I had worn just yesterday. Hope flared in my chest, and I dared not ask—could not bear to hear the answer. No longer caring about privacy, I stripped off the rough uniform and hurried into my dress, nearly weeping at the soft warmth of the material. I placed my filthy feet into my silk slippers and, out of habit, turned my back to the woman so she might tighten my dress.

There was incredulous silence, and I cleared my throat and reached backwards to do it myself. "Where are we going, please?" I asked.

Again, they did not answer. I touched my loose, tangled hair. If they brought me to see someone important, I would look bedraggled and pathetic, but there was nothing to be done. Stepping carefully, gripping my skirts, I was taken down many steps, past hopeless faces that stared at my descent, until I was brought into the dimly lit chamber that served as the Bastille's entry room.

Edgar stood waiting. At my approach, he held his long arms outwards, as if I would rush into them. As if he were my saviour.

I did not move. He lowered his arms, and his expression became mulish. We stared at each other across the small room, a terrible silence throbbing between us like a broken heart. He turned to the guard behind the desk and shook his hand.

"Consider yourself properly warned," the guard said to me. "The next time the gendarmes bring you here, even your husband won't be able to save you."

"I have no husband," I said, meeting the guard's eyes. "My locket, please."

He slid the necklace across the desk to me. My right hand clenched onto the silver chain, the only memento of Alexandre that remained to me. Edgar pushed open the Bastille's heavy door and sunlight blazed, incandescent to my dark-adjusted eyes. I stepped outside with him, to our waiting coach, and despite my best effort, I could not hold back my tears.

The air had never felt sweeter on my skin, the sunlight like a caress from the gods themselves. I inhaled the scent of rust and steel and fresh air—it might have been the first breath in a new set of lungs, for the Mina Kwan I had been was no more.

I was reborn.

My feet skipped across the cobblestone yard, unburdened from the fear I was forced to face in my cell. I ignored Edgar's outstretched hand, fighting the urge to slap it away like a petulant child might, and climbed into the carriage myself.

"You might at least thank me." He sounded wounded. "I

wanted you to see where the occultist's influence would lead you."

I swallowed the hateful responses that seeped into my mouth like bile. There were more important things to say. "I hope you've arranged DuMort's release as well? Or will you just let a good man hang?"

He snorted and looked out the window. "He was to be executed this morning. Somehow, he has escaped. I don't suppose you know anything about that?"

Escaped.

I threw back my head and laughed. Gods and saints, it felt good. Mirth bubbled out of my open mouth, tickling my damaged throat and making my stomach ache. It had been so long.

Edgar's cheeks grew flushed and his eyes darkened with rage. I cared not. I was free of worrying about this man's displeasure, starving for the merest gesture of kindness from him.

Still giggling, I slipped a nail into the locket's clasp and opened it, no longer afraid that it contained a message I would see too late.

There was no note inside, however. There was nothing at all, but a picture of a beautiful DongTi woman, hair held back with an elaborate hair pin, the collar of her dress intricately embroidered. Alexandre's wife wore a demure smile that threatened to grow into a grin, and her eyes were dark and intelligent. She looked familiar.

I brought the locket closer.

It was SuChin.

Chapter Thirteen

I paced the balcony as the sun set, my hair loose and still dripping from my bath. I shivered in the cold air, but I dared not look away from the street. More silver coaches than I'd ever seen filled the avenues, back and forth, scouring the city for their escaped fugitive.

I needed answers that only Alexandre could give me, and I had no idea how to reach him. The gendarmes would be watching his rented apartments, hoping to recapture him, and I could never trust in Edgar's discretion again.

SuChin had died five years ago, if the men I'd sent to search for her could be believed. Sudden and unexpected, they'd said. She had no children, but I hadn't asked about a spouse.

My face burned and I shook my head to dislodge my shameful thoughts. I'd tried to kiss my dead sister's husband. Thank the saints he'd pushed me away.

The saints. My sister was amongst them now, if I hadn't chained her to this earth by talking of her ghost. No wonder Alexandre was so insistent that it wasn't her haunting me: he wished for her to be at peace.

I closed my eyes and whispered into the creeping dusk. "Saints, lead me to where Alexandre DuMort is hiding. I need answers from him."

When I blinked my eyes open, nothing had changed. There were no will-o'-the-wisps to guide me, no star burning bright for me to follow. I remained alone.

If the occultist was smart, he would have fled this cursed city the moment he could. Yet I had a feeling he hadn't. He'd told me that our time was running out, that we had much to accomplish. I could not believe he would abandon whatever secret purpose had brought him here; I could not believe he would abandon *me*.

Think, Mina. Where might he go, trusting me to find him? We had travelled throughout the city for his performances. Those houses might shelter him, as they were accomplices in his crime, but Alexandre would not risk anyone else, not with the gendarmes tearing the city apart for him.

He would go to a place where no one else would be endangered ... a place I would know ... a place with a secret door so neighbours could not see who came and went ...

I grabbed my packed satchel, heavy with gold coin, and a thick, nondescript cloak before hurrying down the stairs.

"Mina? Where are you going?" Edgar demanded from his study. "Have you learned nothing from last night?"

There was no answer to give, nothing left to say. I slammed the front door shut behind me as I left what was once my home, and I strode across the moist grass of my estate, abandoning my wooden wedding band amongst the carefully shorn green carpet.

I hired a passing rickshaw and directed him to the neighbourhood I'd been once before, casting casual glances about me to ensure no one followed us. At the corner, I sent him off and waited for the clack of his wheels on cobblestone to fade before I made my way to the narrow spaces in between houses, into the shadow-filled yards I'd once fled from.

It was difficult to regain my bearings: there were several houses with ivy-covered walls, and so much had happened between that terror-filled night and this one. I did not bring a lantern: it had not occurred to me to bring one, and even the slightest crack of light would blaze like a lighthouse beacon in these shadows. I resigned myself to feeling through the intertwining, leafy coils for the smoothness of a wooden door amongst the bricks. The night was windy and cold, and my traitorous fingers began to numb: as if death itself was spreading towards me, bone by bone, only I was too stubborn to realise it.

A creak of wood in the next house alerted me. I thought it a nosy neighbour and froze, pressing myself tight against the wall, hardly daring to breathe. Another howl of icy wind burned against my exposed cheeks, and the creak sounded again. Hinges.

I headed towards the sound, reaching outwards with my corpse-like hands, and pressed into the dense wall of foliage before me. My fingers sank into this layer of vegetation, continued inwards until I pushed against a door that stood ajar. A moment of panicked binding, as the plants wrapped around me in a ropey embrace, and then I stumbled down the steps of the Wilcox's cellar.

The latch had been broken, no doubt upon someone's rough re-entry. I closed the door firmly and, reaching out blindly, pulled what turned out to be a chair against it. I dared not call out, not yet, not until I knew it was the occultist inside this house rather than a pack of scoundrels. The stairs to the main floor were more or less where I remembered them, and, sweat trickling down my forehead and back, I crept up each step, painstakingly slow.

The house was cold, the air musty and stale. No one had

lit a fire in the hearth nor opened windows for some time. Had the Wilcox's remained in the Dead Thumb's clutches all these weeks? I racked my memory but I could not recall any familiar features amidst the dead-eyed creatures in the cells.

The main floor was brighter than the cellar: the darkness less tangible. Flickering light from the streetlamp outside spilled against the windows, illuminating squares amidst the carefully embroidered curtains. I tread carefully, listening for voices, but there was nothing beyond my own breathing.

The room in which Alexandre had performed was empty, the chairs still lining the walls, except those that had been knocked over in the panic. I looked carefully, at the shadows, remembering how his magnificent gown had fooled my eyes the first time.

In the sitting room, on the couch behind a vase of desiccated flowers, a body rasped its final breaths.

Alexandre.

His eyes blinked open at my approach, and he gave a wan smile. "I hoped you'd find me here, Mina. We are running out of time."

I knelt beside him, searching for injury. He wore only a loose white undershirt untucked from his black pants: even the unsteady light could not hide his disfigured torso. Not just a hunchback: large growths twined around him like a nest of snakes. "I don't understand. Edgar said you escaped."

Alexandre grimaced. "The Society Men took me."

"They saved you?" I could not hide my surprise.

He huffed a laugh: his teeth were stained with blood. "Hardly. They did not wish me to become a martyr by allowing a public execution."

"Where are you hurt?" I was afraid to touch him, unsure if his strange growths were painful. "Should I get help?"

"There is no one that can help us now," Alexandre said. "Mina. There is no time."

"I need answers," I demanded, perhaps cruelly. "I saw SuChin in your locket. All this time, you knew her?"

His exhale rattled, fluids bubbling in his throat. "If you want answers, if you want to save your sister, you must do the unthinkable."

"Save my ... she's—? I'll do it. I'll do anything," I said.

He closed his eyes and nodded. "I thought you would say that. This is the darkest ritual that exists, and we only have one chance to do it. You must gather supplies, and quickly. The concoction of herbs from the red pouch in my gown pocket. A glass of hot water. A clean knife, sharp enough to cut flesh. A leather belt, and a red candle."

I hurried through the house, gathering what the occultist had named. I hesitated when I neared the knives: their blades glinted with promised pain. I grabbed the closest handle and rushed back, carefully depositing each item on the table. His gown was hung over the back of a nearby chair, folded like a shadow touching its toes. For once the material did not move; it lay as still as its owner, something I was grateful for as I searched for the small packet of herbs in one of its many pockets.

Alexandre did not rouse when I returned. I shook his shoulder, the coolness of his skin seeping through the thin material of his undershirt. He did not open his eyes, but he drew another shaky breath.

"The water is not hot, nor fresh," I said, "but I will heat it under the candle flame. The candle is white, not red."

He nodded. "Place the candle beneath my right shoulder blade, under my shirt," he said, and hissed as I obeyed. The candle—and my hand—came back smeared with cold, thick blood. It was imperfect, but I dared not object.

I took the tinderbox from the nearby mantel and nearly moaned with relief when I saw the sulphur-tipped wooden sticks held within: my hands were too sweaty, too shaky, too *bloody* to play with flint and tinder. The acrid smoke seared my nose, but the candle wick caught quickly, filling the room with a golden light of its own.

I held the glass of water, stolen from a bedside table, over the flame until it started to bubble. It did not quite reach a boil, as Alexandre preferred, but I was nervous about the neighbours seeing the candlelight from this abandoned house. I emptied the herbs into the glass and set it aside.

"What now?" I asked. He was taking longer and longer to answer, the gaps between his words stretching longer than a held breath.

"Let it steep, then drink it as fast as you can. It will dull the pain, and prepare the body for what is to come. Hurry. The ritual needs a death, and mine is fast approaching."

I cast a nervous eye at his pallor, at the lack of movement in his chest, and I gulped down the concoction immediately, scalding my mouth and throat. The pain was excruciating: every breath set my scorched tissues newly aflame.

"Where is SuChin?" I wept. "How can I save her? Stay *awake*, Alexandre."

He made a limp attempt to lift his undershirt. I took hold of it and raised it up to his neck, preparing myself for a monstrous sight.

It was even worse than I feared.

My sister stared upward at me, eyes fearful, her head half-emerging from his chest. Their skin was ... joined together, tan and pale complexions melted together like the wax of two candles. She was wrapped around his torso, most of her body partially absorbed into his, with the rest of her sticking outwards like malignant growths.

"Mi Nga," she urged. "Hurry. The ritual cannot be completed without a human death, and Alexandre's time approaches."

I could not dwell on the wonder of hearing her voice for

the first time in decades, nor mourn that my mother was not alive to see this reunion. I followed their instructions even as the herbal drink induced a light-headed fog in my mind, and repeated the strange words SuChin recited. I placed the leather belt in between my teeth and then, taking the knife in my trembling hand, I cut where she told me to cut.

The herbs should have steeped longer: my skin did not numb at all, and I screamed into the rawhide taste of the belt even as I sliced the blade steadily into my ribs. I made a new home for my sister, as my mother had once done for me.

Alexandre did not flinch while I excised his wife from what remained of his body: he did not move at all. They exchanged a long, silent glance as the transfer took place, as she squelched out of his bloody cavity like a newborn and nestled into mine. He looked at me then, and opened his mouth to speak.

What last words he might have said were lost to me, drowned out by the thud of the front door.

The gendarmes had found us.

Chapter Fourteen

The door thudded again, rattling the windows on the side of the house, and wood cracked. I could not move: I was bloodied and sore and light-headed. The image of the Bastille loomed as I whimpered in despair. Even Edgar would not be able to explain why his wife was found performing cursed rituals with the corpse of a wanted man.

SuChin did not hesitate.

She whispered instructions, as though a puppeteer, and I moved to obey them. I slid the knife in between the cushions, and pulled Alexandre's undershirt back down to his waist, before crawling to his black gown and covering myself with it, weeping as the movements pulled at new incisions and brought forth new founts of blood. The herbs were working though: already my bleeding had slowed, and my sister's body fit better in the spaces I had carved for her in my own.

The door burst open at the third blow, and a handful of officers sprinted inside. There was no need to run, I wanted to tell them. The man you seek is beyond further escape.

The first woman stopped at the sight of me, smeared crimson and huddled on the floor. "Where is DuMort?"

I tilted my chin towards the couch.

"Saints above, what happened to him?" she gasped, wide eyes roving over his still form, the blood still seeping through the undershirt I had pulled back down to cover his wounds.

"He ran into some ruffians during his escape," I said, coaxed by SuChin's sibilant whispers, and I did not need to force my tears to flow. "I found him here tonight. It's where we first met." I held up my bloodied hands.

They carried his body away and all but ignored me.

"They think you pathetic," SuChin said, her words hidden to the others beneath the silky rasp of the black gown, the tromping of the gendarmes as they wandered around the room with suspicious eyes. "That you were a hapless fool, too infatuated with him to come to your senses."

Were they wrong?

They left me alone in the house, the door broken open to the frigid wind, the couch stained dark with Alexandre's blood. For a long time, I could not move. Grief overcame me, more potent than any pain, and it was some time before I understood that my body carried SuChin's emotions as well as her flesh.

The bone-deep hunger that gnawed inside me then, the emptiness that made my teeth ache and my fists clench—that was hers, too.

"Before the blood dries, Mi Nga," SuChin said. "Let me eat."

And so I did. I removed the gown and my dress and lay on the floor. My nipples were tipped red with drying blood like a courtesan, while my elder sister licked the sanguine puddle that was all that remained of her husband. I thought of the paper-wrapped package in Alexandre's armoire, the rotten stench that emanated from it, the whiff of the same I'd smelt on Alexandre when he drew near, and I understood what became of the flesh payments he'd demanded for his conduit.

This was to be my responsibility now. My fate. Providing for my sister because she could not do so herself. I gulped the revulsion down the way she did the blood, and thought of how happy my parents would be that we were finally reunited.

When she was sated, I did not pull the gown back into place. I curled on my side on the floor, head bent to my exposed belly. I wanted to relearn her face, the features my failing memories had blurred into nothingness. She was still beautiful, my sister, and I understood why her husband had loved her.

"They said you'd died," I murmured. "The men I hired to find you. Suddenly and unexpectedly."

"I might have, if not for Alexandre," she answered. "It was a difficult birth, and neither I nor my daughter would have survived it."

A wave of fresh grief washed over her—over us—and we fell back into silence, staring into each other's faces the way we used to as children, as we lay in our bed.

Later, as the night began to wane, a thought occurred to me. "I was convinced you were haunting me. It's why I sought out Alexandre in the first place. I believed you meant to kill me."

She shook her head. The movement pulled at our shared flesh, already fused together, the exact same shade so I could not see where her body ended and mine began. "The XieLin had come for you. It killed Father first, and then Mother. And I was content with it haunting me, for it meant you were safe. But once I became—" She shrugged, though only the left shoulder was visible. I could *feel* the other one shifting inside me, nudging at my organs. "—a conduit, as Alexandre called it, half-dead and half-alive, I heard the dead speak. And I knew the spirit was coming for you. And so we travelled here, despite Mydalla's laws, to help you."

"Why didn't you just tell me the truth?" I asked. "We wasted weeks when we could have been together."

"I had hopes ... that Alexandre could teach you about DongTi occultism. That you could use it to survive so you could leave this oppressive city. And I didn't want you to know your sister was a monster, Mi Nga." SuChin frowned. "And now, I have made you a monster too."

We talked and mourned Alexandre and our lost years until dawn broke. SuChin told me to sleep. "We can leave this cursed city tomorrow," she said. "We will make our way around the world, passing on messages from the dead."

"What of the XieLin?" I asked.

"I will keep you safe," my sister answered. She began to sing to me, a song we learned from our mother. It was to that melody I fell asleep.

No longer haunted by past regrets.

No longer afraid of what was to come.

No longer alone.

Bonus Content

A FATE FINER THAN DEATH

I n Mydalla, we do not speak of the dead. They are as saints to us, siphoned into the heavens from our crematoriums' spires, above us fleshly things in all ways. The living, dirt-bound beasts that we are must never call the names of those lost to us, never seek some sign of their continued existence, lest our efforts halt their ascents and doom them to an eternity of suffering.

Like many things our leaders have taught us, this is a lie.

He shrieks himself awake in sweat-sodden sheets for the third time. When he catches his breath, he utters a rasping curse and punches his pillow. From the corner of his darkened chamber, you cover your mouth with your hand and bury your face into my shoulder. You are cool and solid against me, shaking with mirth, and I fling my gratitude to whatever apathetic gods might be listening that we have found each other once more.

~

THE NIGHT of my death (surely I can speak of my own, and if not, what will the constables do about it?), I was not so grateful. I was afraid. One can err in life, and eventually the consequences will end. When one errs in death, however …

I shivered in the shadowed alcove of his front door, while the pre-dawn chill crept into my weary muscles and aching bones. My doubt grew as the hours passed and night waned: perhaps he won't come home tonight; perhaps the ointment stinging my eyes has lost its potency; perhaps, perhaps, perhaps. I checked for the knife hidden in my skirts for the thousandth time, the edge honed like an obsessive purpose, and soothed my mind with my hopes of what was to come.

Slow footsteps approached from down the road. My heart leapt to my throat, nimbler than my numb feet, and I stumbled as I tried to stand. Luck was on my side, for it wasn't him. The streetlamp illuminated a woman's face, bitter with a cruel twist to her mouth, and I exhaled deeply, one worry assuaged. The ointment on my eyes was powerful still: three small shades followed the strange woman like deflated balloons, more proof that all our rituals concerning the dead are meaningless. Despite the laws, punishable by public shaming or worse, the dead do not all pass on. A simple—though hard-learned— recipe of burdock root, dead man's fingers, and turmeric crushed into a paste and applied directly to the whites of the eyes stings like coarse salt and fiery peppers, but will reveal the spirits that remain, bound to the ones who've stripped them of life.

In the months after my discovery, I approached many priests, noblemen, the magistrates themselves: anyone who might hold a modicum of power or influence. None of them listened. Not one of them wanted to know.

Horseshoes clattered against stone. Wood creaked. A carriage drew near. I pressed against his front door, shaking like the delicate leaves providing me cover. He had arrived. Later than I imagined, but he was here.

I fixed your face clearly in my mind, my love for you steeling my nerves, lending mettle to my spine. The man I'd been seeking for two years descended from the carriage steps. After months of handing out bribes and chasing down unfounded rumors, trading information for ointment and other small crafts, he was finally before me. A wide-shouldered, handsome thing, wearing a tailored suit and carrying a gentleman's cane. Could my sources have been mistaken?

Doubt vanished a moment afterwards. My fading memory of your face was no longer necessary to grant me courage: I just had to use my burning eyes. As the tall man stumbled up the cobblestone path to his door, you appeared behind him. And not just you. A chain of silent, diaphanous women trailed in the nobleman's wake like nervous brides. The vision of you wavered as I fought back tears, swallowed sobs. But this was no time for emotion.

The carriage driver pulled away. The streets were dark, and your killer was drunk. I stepped from the shadows to stop him from reaching the door, knife loose in my hand.

He startled at the sight of me, swaying, eyes crossing to focus on my dark form. "What do you want, then?" he slurred.

"Nothing from you," I said. "I'm here for Ren." Despite Mydalla's laws, I called your name.

You did not look up at the sound of my voice. Only your killer's lurch backward earned your attention, tethered to him as you were. Drunk and surprised as he was, he avoided my pathetic attack with ease. It took mere seconds for him to disarm me. Before the night's chill could separate us, I threw all my strength, my fury, my grief, into grabbing ahold of his wide fist. His fist, which still gripped my sharp knife, I pulled towards me, into my own throat.

The blade was a red-hot poker singeing my skin. My blood, my air, escaped from the hole in my throat like steam from doused steel. I called your name with numbing lips as I fell.

This time, you heard me. "Beth!" You crouched at my side, eyes wide, the touch of your hands cool. "What have you done?"

"Don't leave me," I said, an echo of a more painful time.

"Never," you promised, gripping my limp hand within both of yours.

Your killer—now mine—stood above my dying body with furious eyes. He launched a kick into my sternum that broke ribs, cursed his poor luck, and raised his voice to call for his servants.

I stared into your eyes as my life passed before mine.

LIFE IS MEASURED BY EVENTS, by memories that make and break us. The summer nights of our childhoods, warm and sticky, when you soothed me while I cried at the pain of my father's anger upon me, holding me as fireflies flared like dying stars around us. The Autumn day you were to marry Tomas, and we pledged our eternal friendship, witnessed by falling leaves that shushed us to silence. The cold December day I found you lying on the wooded path to my house, I thought you were making snow angels in the gentle powder of the year's first snowfall—until I saw the scarlet wings spreading from your yawning throat.

I held your hand while your blue eyes searched the sky before focusing on mine. "Don't leave me," you whispered, the second mouth in your throat bubbling with blood.

"I won't," I'd vowed. "Who did this to you?"

You left me then. Left me grieving, and lost, and enraged.

The constable that eventually came declared you Ascended and deemed your name unutterable. He looked down at me as he said this, benevolently, as if expecting my gratitude. As if death was a mercy to people such as us, those who survived on the edges of civilized society working for crumbs.

Once news spread, other friends celebrated on your behalf, raised cheap glasses of wine skyward and sighed with envy. Even Tomas forced a smile through his tears and threw his wedding band into the tavern fire. "May we find one another again," he said, but even that drew disapproving glares from eavesdroppers. He slipped away as the wooden ring burned, smoke drifting up the ash-stained flue like ghosts.

As long as the nobleman lives, doors will always creak open; his nightmares will be full of blood; and sourceless voices will whisper taunts into his ears. He has grown gaunt and grey with our mischiefs, a fate his hands have denied us. I pray he has a long life: decades Ren and I have to spend together, decades he'd robbed from us. The murderer can afford physicians and herbalists that will sustain him into old age, even as he cannot tell them what truly haunts him.

In Mydalla, the living do not speak of the dead.

But the dead—we speak to each other.

Acknowledgments

I'm very grateful to Antonia Ward, owner of Ghost Orchid Press, for giving my little gaslamp horror a chance, and for being exceptionally nice, understanding, and on top of things throughout this process. I'm also grateful to Ed Crocker for making the editing process so easy, and to Faera Lane for creating the stunning cover that captured DuMort's vibe so well.

This novella passed through many hands before it was published: many thanks to Chris O'Halloran, Jolie Toomajan, Tim Bloom, Brett Mitchell Kent, Jim Doran, and Kelsea Yu for blurbing DuMort, and for always being so supportive.

I also want to thank my family: my hard-working parents who immigrated to Canada to give their kids a better life, my sisters who are steady sources of support, and Billy, Jake, and Gracie for encouraging me and giving me the time to write.

And I am most grateful to God for the many blessings in my life.

Michelle Tang
April 2025

Michelle Tang was born in Manila, Philippines, and immigrated as a child to Canada. She's a nurse, marathon napper, and video game addict, who scribbles down stories in her spare time. *DuMort* is her debut novella, and her debut novel will be released in the summer of 2026. You can find Michelle at her website, https://michelletangwrites.wixsite.com/author.

www.ingramcontent.com/pod-product-compliance
Lightning Source LLC
Chambersburg PA
CBHW010320100726
47906CB00006B/1063